M000207880

# *Horse Dreams*

# *Horse Dreams*

MARY VIVIAN JOHNSON

TATE PUBLISHING
AND ENTERPRISES, LLC

*Horse Dreams*
Copyright © 2013 by Mary Vivian Johnson. All rights reserved.

No part of this publication may be reproduced, stored in a retrieval system or transmitted in any way by any means, electronic, mechanical, photocopy, recording or otherwise without the prior permission of the author except as provided by USA copyright law.

Reprinted by permission of Al-Anon Family Group Headquarters, Inc. Excerpts from Al-Anon Conference Approved Literature are reprinted with permission of Al-Anon Family Group Headquarters, Inc. Permission to reprint these excerpts does not mean that Al-Anon Family Group Headquarters, Inc. has reviewed or approved the contents of this publication, or that Al-Anon Family Group Headquarters, Inc. necessarily agrees with the views expressed herein. Al-Anon is a program of recovery for families and friends of alcoholics—use of these excerpts in any non Al-Anon context does not imply endorsement or affiliation by Al-Anon.

The opinions expressed by the author are not necessarily those of Tate Publishing, LLC.

Published by Tate Publishing & Enterprises, LLC
127 E. Trade Center Terrace | Mustang, Oklahoma 73064 USA
1.888.361.9473 | www.tatepublishing.com

Tate Publishing is committed to excellence in the publishing industry. The company reflects the philosophy established by the founders, based on Psalm 68:11,
*"The Lord gave the word and great was the company of those who published it."*

Book design copyright © 2013 by Tate Publishing, LLC. All rights reserved.
*Cover design by Rodrigo Adolfo*
*Interior design by Mary Jean Archival*

Published in the United States of America

ISBN: 978-1-62563-830-4
1. Fiction / General
2. Fiction / Family Life
13.04.04

# *Dedication*

I dedicate this writing
    to my sister, my brother,
    my nieces, my nephews,
    my daughters, my husband,
    and countless others I've known and loved
    who long for the innocence of their childhood.
    We all look forward to a happy ending.

In memory of Mom and Dad…
    I love you with all my heart,
    and I forgive you to the depths of my soul.
    I pray these words reach across time and space
    so that eternally you might find it in your hearts
    to do the same for me.

# *Acknowledgments*

The people who surround a writer—especially their spouses, family, and friends—are special people. My thanks and dearest love goes out to each and every one of you.

To all my newest friends at Tate Publishing, thank you for your patience and step-by-step gentle guidance through this grand "ride."

I would like to thank Lucinda for her inspiration to take up writing again, for her kind ear, and especially for the colors of the rainbow she brought to this story and to my life.

To my neighbors Ken and your dear mother Nancy, Joy, Mary, and Dorothy and my new friends Cindy and Wade, Elaine and Denny, those who have guided me through the scary waters of change and helped me to find new purpose in my life; you're teaching me how to *love my neighbors as myself.*

To Shirley and everyone in the WOW group, thank you for your constant encouragement and reminders to keep in the Word.

To Marilyn, I am in deep gratitude for your friendship and the priceless gift of allowing me to photograph Trouble and put an actual face to my character Medallion.

To Cynthia Leitich Smith for your expertise and your reminder, "You can only succeed if you decide not to give up."

To Becky, Ron, Mike, Susan, Kenneth, Allen, Amy, Kelly, and Patrick, thank you for your inspiration and hugs.

To Beth for her profound encouragement after the first five chapters when she said, "Where's the rest? I need more."

To Pam and Jim, Chance, Chase, and Chandler who gave up their time long ago at a family reunion to help with revision and inspiration.

To Emily and Tad, Chloe and Christian, Jenny and Nick, Vivian and Isaac, you light up my life more than you'll ever know.

Most especially, I give thanks to and for my dear horseman, my first editor, and the love of my life for his patience, expertise, and love…Thanks, Johnny.

Of course, it goes without saying, but cannot be withheld, all praise, honor, and glory goes to the Lord our God, without whom nothing exists except by His Holy Word.

> *[The Lord] will cover you with his feathers,*
> *and under his wings you will find refuge;*
> *his faithfulness*
> *will be your shield and rampart.*
>
> *Psalm 91:4*

# *Contents*

## *Insanity Reigns*

Thunder rumbled in the distance, and a thick gray cloud swirled overhead, doubling in size. I stared straight into Dad's eyes and, without blinking, said, "I'm not a baby, Dad. Please let me see my horse…now."

The shadows grew deeper as I turned and walked past Dad through the doorway of the barn. A bolt of lightning flashed, the thunder booming on its heels. A chill shuttered down my spine. Once my eyes adjusted to the dark, I focused on a gated stall near the back where my horse snorted and neighed and pounded angry hooves against the wall.

"Medallion!" I yelled out his name, slowing my pace to the gate. The commotion in the stall ceased. I crept forward three more steps. Dad and our friend John followed close behind. The horse froze in the middle of the stall, a shadow with perked ears. He waited, blowing one hesitant snort in my direction.

With gentleness this time, I repeated his name, "Medallion." The palomino eased cautiously to the gate. A dim light filtered in from the stable entrance, giving me the first glimpse of my horse's face.

From the shadows, his eye met mine. My heart burned like an arrow, shot straight through to my soul. Thunder rumbled low, moved from one side of the sky to the other, strangely comforting this time like a powerful yet kind arm encircling me.

"Oh God," I begged, knowing His Spirit alone could fill in the unspoken words of my heart-wrenching prayer.

Suddenly my breath caught, my head felt dizzy, and my knees quivered ready to give way. I steadied myself with one shaky hand on the cool iron bar of the gate. With the other hand, I reached up to touch the spongy cushion of my horse's muzzle.

Blood trickled onto my fingers, gushing from a fresh skin-ripped gash just below Medallion's withered white star. I smelled the stench of it in the humid air of the barn and swallowed back a surge of vomit that rose to my chest as Medallion blew warm air into the palm of my hand.

Dad opened another door leading to the outside. More light, charged by occasional flashes of lightning, penetrated the air of the stable giving me a better look at my horse. A small breath of air from the open door helped to clear my head, and John steadied my shoulders with a strong tender hand.

A ruler-size slit across Medallion's chest also oozed blood. His left leg was bandaged from a previous incident. Numerous cuts crisscrossed his mud-crusted golden side. His mane was matted and both it and his tail had chunks of hair sliced from them.

Medallion no longer resembled the innocent "little pony" from my youth but rather a beast I hardly recognized. I realized perhaps for the first time some adult decisions were going to be very difficult to make.

Being forced to leave Medallion in San Antonio all those months ago had hurt so much. I lived through it. But now the fear of losing my horse forever terrified me, and I wasn't sure that I could go on.

The rain began to drain the clouds, and I shuddered, feeling more alone than I had in months.

## *The Momentous Day*

My tenth birthday, two years ago…The day will be forever branded on my mind.

It started out with a spotlight aimed straight at my eye, that big old moon, shining in through the curtain. Beautiful really.

I jumped up and tiptoed to the window to take a better look. The moon hung full and bright, like a rare pearl, suspended in the folds of a cold velvet sky. My first gift in what surely promised to be a momentous day.

A chill pinched my arms. I crept over to the rocking chair and grabbed a red checkered quilt Grandma had made and sent for my birthday. As I threw it around my shoulders, a twinge of sadness squeezed my heart. When I called yesterday to thank Grandma, she said she and Grandpa wouldn't be coming down for my party. "You'll have far too many friends around to miss a couple of old fogies like us."

I hated to admit it, but she was probably right. Though I would miss them, Grandma and Gramps had grown so old-fashioned these days. I much preferred going shopping and hanging out with my friends.

With the quilt around my arms, I padded to the kitchen for my usual glass of orange juice. That's when I noticed Dad asleep on the couch. Odd. It seemed to me I'd seen him there a couple of times that week. He was snoring so loudly the rafters jiggled. Smiling, I shrugged my shoulders and tiptoed past my parents' closed bedroom door. No wonder Mom shooed him out of there.

As usual, she was still asleep and would stay that way for at least a couple more hours. Saturdays were her only days to sleep in. Besides, when I got through Facebooking last night, she and Dad were still up talking. Rare. They didn't do that much lately.

I closed the refrigerator and poured my orange juice. As I stood sipping it, I pulled back the curtain and looked through the kitchen window across the street to the field where we kept my horse. That moon shed its light directly over Medallion's barn. Suddenly, I had an idea, a little bit daring, but wasn't that what birthdays were supposed to be, a chance to stretch our wings a bit?

Quickly, I threw on my jeans and T-shirt and slipped out the back door. Sneaking out at daybreak, pure adrenaline coursed through my veins. With that moon as full as a floodlight on one side of the sky and brilliant pink fingers now stretching over the horizon on the other side, I easily made my way across the empty road between our house and Medallion's fenced pasture.

He heard the gate clink open and started snorting and stomping in his stall. I skipped through the barn, into the tack room where his saddle was resting on the saddle rack. That antiquated monster was way too heavy for me to lift. So I left it and reached for the bridle. At least Dad had taken the time to teach me how to put that on Medallion. I was getting pretty good at it too as long as the horse stood still and lowered his head for me.

His ears perked to attention as my boots scuffed across the stable floor. I raised my hand to greet him, and his flared nostrils blew warm air against my palm. Tickling my hand, his muzzle searched for food. But it wasn't time to eat. I was determined to take my first solo ride.

"We'll eat later, boy," I whispered. "Right now, you've got to take this bit in your mouth, so we can get a ride in before anyone wakes up." He fought me for a while, jerking his head up and down. But I took my time, rubbing the white star hidden underneath the hair between his ears. Finally he lowered his head and let me slip the bit into his mouth.

Normally, I would've spent some time brushing Medallion, calming him down for the ride. But I'd groomed him well the night before, and I needed to get him up and going.

Without the saddle's stirrup to put my foot in, the horse would be hard to mount. So I led him over to the stall gate where I climbed up and slipped right onto his back.

Trotting out of the barn and into the closed corral, I could feel Medallion's powerful muscles under my knees. He stomped the ground, snorting and antsy to go. As I nudged him up to speed, the crisp morning air stung my cheeks and caused my eyes to water. I swiped the tears away and grabbed the reins tighter in my hands. Giving the stallion a gentle heel, I clicked, "Giddyap."

His muscles tightened as he lunged forward into a strong lope. I circled once on the familiar path inside the corral like Dad and I had practiced. But this day, I wanted more. I wanted to run with the wind, free in the open pasture, outside the protected confines of the corral.

"Whoa, boy. Hold on, boy," I repeated, struggling a bit with Medallion's reins and finally pulling him to a stop. He pawed the ground as I leaned over to unlatch the chain that released the gate.

Taking a deep breath, I aimed him out, into the wide grassy field where we could run free, then heeled him gently with my boot. The power beneath me surged. Away we galloped, his hooves pelting the ground. My heart raced like it did last summer when I rode the pitching Superman Krypton Roller Coaster at Fiesta Texas.

Up to the top of a hill we sped where the old oak spread its branches and patches of bluebonnets painted the hills a rich sea of blue. I circled around the oak and reined Medallion in. Surveying the land below, I glimpsed our house, peaceful in the distance. The gentle Texas wind whipped a loose strand of hair across my lips as I paused to catch my breath.

After a few seconds, I urged the stallion again with my legs and down the hill we raced. Like the roller coaster, Medallion lunged. Through the field he ran, whipping me here and there on a couple of daring hairpin turns. I positioned Medallion beside the ranch's straight fence line and the road next to it, and along we sped. Cars on the other side motored along behind us, sluggishly beginning their early morning routines.

Abruptly, out of nowhere, a motorcycle roared up on the road next to the fence. From the corner of my eye, I saw his black helmet gleam as the rider hunched down low and gunned his engine. He swerved closer, squealing his back tire, challenging us to pit motor against beast.

I knew better than to do anything so foolish. Blaring motorcycles and horses certainly don't mix. I tried to slow Medallion back to a trot. The horse, however, had a mind of his own and was not to be outdone.

Like a fireball, Medallion bolted forward in a dead-out uncontrollable run. I fought with the reins and, leaning forward, clutched handfuls of mane, all the while yelling, "Whoa! Whoa! Stop!"

Fence posts blurred beside us. Holding tightly to his mane, I saw the ground flying by as we quickly barreled toward the barn. My mind darted from one question to another. Should I jump? Are we going to slam into the barn? What if he stops and throws me over his head? "My God!" I called out. "Help me!" With all my might, I held on and clinched the horse's sides with my knees.

God heard my prayer. Suddenly, Medallion's legs locked up and he slid, stopping just inches from the corner of the barn.

As the Medallion roller-coaster ride careened to a stop, my chest was thrown against the horse's neck, jolting my hips upward almost over my head, then slamming my tailbone back down against the hard bone of Medallion's back. I grimaced in pain and collapsed against Medallion's neck. We were both breathing hard, now soaked with sweat.

Shaking, I climbed off, slipping down his wet coat the last few inches to the ground. As my toes touched the grass, my knees buckled beneath me. I dropped hard, striking my tender tailbone again, this time against the edge of a rock. Excruciating pain shot up my spine.

I let go of the reins, and Medallion trotted off to graze in a nearby patch of grass as if nothing at all had happened.

I, on the other hand, lay crumpled on the ground gasping for breath. A picture of Superman, Christopher Reeve, paralyzed as he was the last days of his life from the neck down flashed through my mind, and fear gripped my chest.

As quickly as I could, I wobbled to my hands and knees, thanking God that I could move. Slowly inching my way up all the way to my feet, I took a couple of steps to make sure I could still walk. Miraculously, I ended up with only a slight bruise to my tailbone; however, my confidence was badly shaken. I always felt so safe and secure, in complete control of my life, until today.

Medallion allowed me to limp over and pick up his reins. He acted as docile as a two-ticket ride at the neighborhood Kiddie Acres pony farm. But I knew I would never look at him quite the same way as I had. He was no longer just a pretty pony. He now commanded from me more respect. Horses are powerful animals, and I had learned in these fleeting moments, just how quickly tables could turn.

Slowly, I walked Medallion back to the barn and replaced the bridle with his halter. I washed him down and brushed the sweat from his golden sides. Several minutes passed. My heartbeat finally returned to normal as I combed Medallion's mane back to corn silk.

Just then, Dad strolled over to the stall, his morning cup of coffee steaming in his hand. "You sure have done a beautiful job cleaning the old boy up, darlin'. You about ready for your morning ride?"

I sighed, tossing Medallion's brush back into a bucket. *I may never ride again*, I thought. But I answered casually, "No, Dad. It's getting kind of late. I think I'll just get ready for my birthday party." As I limped away, I felt his curious eyes following me all the way back across the street.

## *Party on the River*

Oh man, was my bottom ever sore as we rode in the car later that Saturday afternoon. We were headed over to the Rivercenter Mall in downtown San Antonio. I sat on one hip, then painfully rose up on my hands, and switched over to the other hip to keep from sitting full center on my bruised tailbone. I didn't complain though, number one because I felt lucky just to be able to sit at all. And number two because this little incident had to remain a big secret.

Besides, my tenth birthday party, the party of a lifetime, was just about to begin. Dad pulled into slot E-2 in the parking garage, and he and Mom discussed what level we were on, so they could be sure and find the car when we were ready to leave.

As we entered the mall, I spotted a Dippin Dots Ice Cream stand. "Look, Dad! Can we all get some Dippin Dots later before we leave for the hotel?"

"Sure, pumpkin," he answered me without hesitation. But Mom slashed out at him with a look of murder in her eyes, muttering under her breath about the cost of an ice cream per child times twenty-five.

"I'm sorry, Mom," I whispered. "I didn't think about the expense. You guys are already paying for so much. I shouldn't even have suggested that."

It was true. In addition to the price of renting out the party barge with a full-course Mexican lunch for twenty-five of my friends, Dad also said the girls could each have twenty dollars to buy a little something for their party favor. Then later that evening, three "best friends" and I were being treated to the best hotel room on the River Walk at the La Mansion del Rio for a slumber party.

Mom had already hit the roof more than once about all the extravagance. She was clearly at the end of her rope. But instead of launching into her usual sermon about unrealistic spending for working-class people, she just bowed her head and bit her bottom lip, quiet but totally frustrated.

Then she did something that I really hate. She pulled me into what felt like an hour-long bear hug right in the middle of the mall! I tore myself out of her arms but not before my "best friends" approached, laughing and pointing from around the corner.

"Hi, Bec," called Sue Ann. She was the closest real-life Barbie that I ever knew, even down to her quickly developing body and the silky blond hair, which flowed all the way down her back. And here she was walking straight up to me with her best friends, Amy and Jan, closely following one step behind her. "How sweet," she said sarcastically, looking at Mother, then at me, her words dripping with sugar.

I remember thinking in that moment…And I call her my friend because? But I knew why. I secretly wanted to be just like her. Who wouldn't want to be? She had the Gap shopping bags, the look of a *Teen Vogue* model, and the popularity. That's why these three girls were the ones I'd invited to join me later in the evening at the hotel for the private slumber party.

As we walked to the landing and met up with all the other friends joining us on the barge, Mom tried to point out the band serenading the crowd and other interesting things in the garden along the banks of the San Antonio River. But no one listened to her. We were way too busy practicing "the walk" and doing "the talk" to notice anything so mundane as the River Walk, better known by locals as "the crown jewel of Texas."

All I could hear were Sue Ann's words, "I can't wait till this boat moves on down the river away from that band and all their racket." And so we did.

When Dad first told me his idea of going on the barge, I thought it sounded fun. We could feed the ducks nacho bits like we used to do as a family. And my friends would all pay attention to me like my family used to do.

It didn't quite work out that way though. All talk centered around Sue Ann and what "she said, he said" and "who said what and where and how much." Then she turned bored and wondered out loud, "What are we going to do next? I'm tired of just hanging around this old nasty river."

The girls only paid attention to me when Mom and Dad started arguing later that night in the living room of the hotel suite.

I break out into a sweat even today as I think about how humiliated I felt that night.

We were in the bedroom talking about Sue Ann's latest boyfriend when suddenly everyone grew deathly still. They were all staring at me as they listened to Mom yell, "Why do you have to spend so much?"

Then Dad yelled back, "Why do you have to nag so much? You know the divorce is final, and this is the last time we will do anything as a family, so just let it alone!"

My heart stopped, then I grew light-headed as the power of Dad's words thrust daggers at my chest, "Divorce…the last time we will do anything as a family…" and if that wasn't bad enough, it was yelled out in front of my "best friends." At that moment, I wanted to crawl into the nearest hole. But before going down, I displayed my last ounce of courage.

Shutting the bedroom door behind me, I padded into the living room, dressed in ridiculous pink shaggy slippers and whispered to my parents, "Is there something you'd like to say to me in private, *besides* happy birthday?"

But all they could do is lower their eyes in silence. The truth had already escaped from their lips.

# Friends

Monday afternoon when I got home from school, I threw my backpack on the bed, grabbed an apple, and headed across the street to Medallion. Needless to say, this day turned out to be a real pain in the…tailbone.

I'd hoped to keep all the party mess a secret, but as I was soon to learn, my so-called "best friends" thought the whole school ought to know every detail of my private life.

I should have known the wildfire was already raging because every hallway I walked through had groups of kids laughing until I approached. Then the gossip stopped, went stone quiet until I passed by, and then the snickering resumed.

Turns out my best friends fired up Facebook as soon as we dropped them off at their homes on Sunday. And as if that didn't fan the flame fast enough, they came in early Monday and started flapping their lips before the first bell rang. By lunch, my life read like a tabloid headline, *Momentous River Walk Birthday Fiasco Ends in Split of the Becky Harris Family.*

Of course, the one being talked about is usually the last to know.

Mrs. Lipstick droned on and on all morning about "cause and effect" or something boring like that. I really don't know what she was talking about since I had so many of my own thoughts thrashing around in my head.

Lunch time finally crawled around. I was anxious to sit with my friends and talk about something other than the divorce or cause and effect.

I saw Sue Ann and headed for her table. But as I was about to put my tray down, she waved her hand in kind of a loopty-loop and said, "All these seats are taken." Sure enough, four of the other girls I'd invited to my birthday party pushed me aside and quickly filled in the spots. Most of the other girls I'd invited were also already in their established pods.

I walked on and saw Tommy Anderson and all the cool guys seated together at the guy table. Tommy gave me a smirk, then turned, and laughed out loud to the fellows sitting around him.

The only seats left were at the invisible table, the table where each kid takes his own spot and sits with other invisibles on either side, the only quiet table in the cafeteria.

I noticed Irene sitting there, so I aimed for her. But even she ducked her head and quickly went back to her library book like she was mad at me.

Irene had moved into our neighborhood when we were both in second grade. Back then, I sought out new kids or those who looked lonesome, trying to make them feel welcome. Now that I was older, in the fifth grade, I didn't do that much anymore.

Groups had already formed by fifth grade. I categorized myself to be in the "not exactly" group, not exactly popular, not exactly not.

The popular group was rich. I was not in that group, but not in the poor group either. The rich group dressed in all the latest fashions while my fashion had to be rated as "not exactly," mostly *Tarjay* look-alikes.

I didn't behave like the populars either; well, not exactly. I wondered sometimes if these girls had a conscience. They could be downright mean and cruel, like they had treated me just seconds before at the lunch table. I couldn't do that, at least not on purpose.

As I sat picking the crust off my sandwich, I tried to remember how I treated Irene at the party on Saturday. I hadn't invited her to the special slumber party. But of course I had invited her to the lunch on the barge. I'd known her for a long time.

On the barge, there were twenty-five friends. I tried to remember if she was there. With shame, I realized I couldn't even remember if she was or not. She was, well, invisible to me.

"Uh, Irene," I attempted conversation to find out if she had come. "Do you like the River Walk?" Not *did* you like the River Walk? That would imply she was in fact there, which I did not know.

"Sure," she answered quietly. "I especially like it at Christmas when they have it all lit up. My mom always takes me to the River Walk. She says it reminds her of Venice."

*Good*, I thought. *At least we were talking*. By what she had just said, I still didn't know if she was at the party, but at least we were talking, and she mentioned something interesting. That was the thing I really like about Irene. She always said interesting things, probably because she reads so much.

"What are you reading?" I ventured, going in another direction.

"*Dear Mr. Henshaw*," she answered quietly. "I thought it might be good to read it again…maybe it could give me something helpful to say to you, what with the divorce and all. Sue Ann's *first* Facebook entry about everything was sent to all of us on the barge."

Yep, she was there. My mortification was complete, and I certainly wasn't ready to talk about it. So I just answered, "Yeah." Then I lowered my head and silently refocused on ripping the remaining crust from my bread.

Later that evening I muddled through all that was in my mind as I entered the barn and trudged across the floor. Medallion heard me approach and whinnied a warm welcome. I unlatched the door to his stall, and he ambled over straight into my waiting arms. He lowered his head, and I kissed the star on his forehead, realizing he was truly my only real friend. With him, I was convinced I didn't need anyone else.

## *My Only Friend*

Tuesday, my first day as the *invisible* girl, began with a weather report from a way-too-chipper radio forecaster, "Today will be cloudy with a chance of showers right around lunchtime." *Perfect*, I thought. Sifting through a rainbow of clothes hanging in the closet, nothing suited my mood until finding my old comfortable black sweater. I dressed in silence and then slipped out the back door to catch the bus before Mom got up. It was a relief to escape the house where everything had become as silent as a cemetery.

At least at school math problems had real solutions that I could actually figure out. People laughed there, too, even if I wasn't one of them. I had decided to no longer try and fit in with the populars. Every time I glimpsed one of them, I ducked my head, unable to look into their eyes for fear they would either ignore me like I wasn't there or come right out and laugh at me.

In class, it was easy to be invisible: just keep quiet, look down, and appear lost in my work. The only real difficult part of the day was lunch where I had usually hung out and joked with my friends. Now I would remain at the invisible table. That suited me just fine. I could safely burrow underground and hide inside the covers of a book. It didn't matter to anyone whether I concentrated on the words or just zoned out and stared at them. Behind the pages, I saw no one gawking at me or judging my life.

The hours of the day dragged on in silence until I hopped off the afternoon bus and headed for the barn. A beam of sunlight broke through the clouds to warm my shoulders. I unloaded the heavy backpack and tossed it to a nearby hay bale. Finally I felt free to talk with my only friend.

"Medallion, come here, boy," I called from the barn. Just seeing him grazing in the pasture among the bluebonnets lifted my spirits. I got a bucket of oats and headed out across the field. He saw me and whinnied hello, then raised his tail, and loped to meet me halfway.

I pulled an apple I had saved from lunch out of my sweater pocket and crunched a bite, just as Medallion skidded up to me. "You want the rest, big guy?" I asked him.

"Of course," he nickered. Then he finished it off, core and all, in one juicy chomp. He loved apples, so I was sure to bring him one every time I came over to see him. After eating the apple, he allowed me to easily hook the lead rope onto his halter. Then we walked to the barn for his afternoon grooming.

The spring sunshine warmed Medallion's golden coat, reminding me of the fresh loaves of bread Mom used to bake. The horse's shaggy winter hair was beginning to slough off. As summer approached, his coat would start to shimmer like gold. As I brushed his side, I remembered how Medallion got his name.

The night after Dad had bought the horse, our family was watching the summer Olympics on TV. During a medal presentation, Dad shouted, "That's it! Your horse can be called Medallion, Medallion the Stallion." I thought it sounded a little dorky at first. At age eight, however, I was kind of into rhymes, so after I said it a couple of times, the name sort of clicked for me.

"Medallion," I repeated the name as I brushed through his long white mane. "That name still fits you perfectly, doesn't it, boy?"

He neighed in agreement, nodding his head, then proudly held it up high. "That's right, it's a proud name, isn't it? A name fit for a winner."

I brushed the hair between his ears. He held them straight up, perked to attention.

"We had quite a ride Saturday," I whispered, looking up into his eyes, holding the secret just between the two of us. "I have to admit you scared me, but still, we were as free as the wind, weren't we, boy?"

He nickered again, pawing at the sawdust on the barn floor. He seemed antsy to run again. But with the mood over at the house the way it was, I didn't want to do anything to draw attention to myself.

Dad hadn't wasted any time moving out. On our way back home Sunday after the birthday fiasco, the tension was so thick in the car that it made my stomach wrench into knots.

No sooner had he jerked the car into park, Dad bolted straight to the bedroom, gathered up two suitcases he obviously had already packed, then stormed outside and threw them into his truck.

"Beg him to stay if that's what you want," Mom commanded me from the kitchen cabinet where she stood.

I followed him out of the house. He stopped his retreat only for a second to give me a quick hug.

"I hate good-byes," he whispered with tears in his eyes. "Don't worry, hon, I'll keep in touch." Then he turned, jumped into the seat, slammed the door, and sped off, squealing the tires behind him.

I had done absolutely nothing to stop him, no begging, no crying, no trying to reason with him. It happened so quickly; all I could do was stand there in shock, shaking like a scared, silent rabbit.

Now that Dad had moved out, Mom and I were on our own. I'd have to be really careful not to get hurt or cause any kind of trouble. Mom had a lot on her mind. She sure didn't need me causing anymore grief. I already felt guilty.

"Do you think it was my fault that they split up?" I asked Medallion. "I don't mean to make *you* feel bad, but it could've been because of both of us. After all, you remember how mad Mom got when Dad brought you home."

I still remember the way she yelled at Dad, "You bought a stallion? A stallion? For an eight-year-old? What were you thinking?

But even back then, I knew I was big enough. So what if you were a little spirited, what was the big whoop about that?

"Becky, time for dinner," Mom yelled from across the street.

"Oh well, at least she let me keep you," I whispered, kissing my friend on the nose. I dropped Medallion's brushes in the bucket and put him in his stall for the night.

"Good night, big guy. Sure glad I've got you to talk to. See you in the morning." He nickered his reply as I plodded over to the house, just in time to catch the latest scene in "As the Divorce Turns."

# As the Divorce Turns

As I walked in the door, I heard the TV blasting away. Mom was watching an old-time soap opera that she taped every day to watch when she got home from work. I thought the show was stupid, a bunch of grown-ups kissing then fighting, then kissing again. And it went on day after day, the same old plot, only with the characters all changing places and kissing different people.

Mom sat in the recliner, Dad's old recliner, with her feet propped up and a glass of wine in her hand. When I came in, she brought her glass with her and set it down on the dining room table. Then she went in the kitchen and served us both up a heap of macaroni and cheese. I poured myself a glass of milk and took my usual place at the table. Mom took Dad's place at the head of the table, as far away from me as she could.

After an awkward silence, she started eating and I joined her, leaving our usual evening prayer unsaid. As she ate and stared right past me at the TV, I tried to tell her about my day. "I had kind of a hard day today, especially at lunch when…"

But I stopped midsentence because she hadn't heard a single word I had said. There was a blank expression on her face. She just kept staring straight ahead.

This was certainly a big turnaround. Before, Mom had always questioned me about my day. But now, she seemed in a daze, totally into herself, just drinking her wine and staring at that TV. And there it was again, this overwhelming feeling that I was sinking down into the empty world of the invisible. I fought to pull myself up out of it.

Maybe if I changed the subject Mom would start talking. So I sat up and brightly asked, "When will Dad be coming over to clean out Medallion's stall?"

Boy oh boy, I had her attention then! She turned and looked at me with steel in her eyes. "Your dad's not coming back, Rebecca, so just get used to it. You and I are both going to have to carry a lot more weight around here. Now as far as that horse goes, if you want it, you've got to clean up after it."

With that, she swiped up her plate of macaroni, took it to the kitchen, and slid it across the counter. So much for talking. She poured herself another glass of wine, took it directly to her bedroom, slammed the door, and didn't come out for the rest of the night.

I washed off the dishes and stored the rest of the macaroni in the refrigerator. Then I sneaked off to my own room and tried to concentrate on a reading assignment Mrs. Lipstick had given to us. Needless to say, that was hopeless. I reread the same paragraph at least four times, then went ahead through the next two pages, only to find out at the end I had no idea what the chapter was about. So much for homework.

By eight o'clock, after all the rehashing my brain had done, sifting through the guilt I felt about Medallion, and repressing all the anger I was beginning to feel toward my mother, my eyelids felt like they had weights attached to them. I could do nothing more than curl up in a ball on my bed and go to sleep. That seemed my only relief.

Before I knew it, the midmorning sun was streaming into my bedroom. I awoke, startled by the realization, for the first time in my life, I was late for school. Quickly I ran to the bathroom, swept my hair back in a ponytail, and threw on some clean clothes. I knocked on Mom's door to get a tardy note to take to school, but she wouldn't answer.

Opening the door, I found her still asleep, curled on top of the covers still in her clothes from yesterday. A twinge of sympathy tugged at my heart as I gently tapped her shoulder and whispered, "Mom, Mom, I'm late for school."

Accidentally, my shoe clinked against an empty wine bottle that lay on the floor next to Mom's bed. She groggily opened her eyes. They were puffy and red. I realized she was in no shape to drive. So I kissed her on the cheek and then slipped out, quietly closing the door behind me. Since I had to have a note to get into class, I scribbled one out for myself and guiltily signed Mom's name. This would be only the first in a long line of times that I would have to cover for her. And such became the pattern of our new lives.

## Disappearing Dad

I t was almost as if someone waved a magic wand over my dad and said, "Abracadabra." He simply disappeared. When I asked Mom where he was, she replied, "Finding himself." So without him in our lives, we now had to find ourselves as well.

One good thing I found out about myself is that I could step up to bat when I needed to do so. Dad had always been the one to feed and clean up after Medallion. But since he wasn't around, Mom left this responsibility up to me. So every morning, I'd dish out the oats and separate and distribute the proper amount of hay for the day. The troughs had to be kept full of clean water, which meant dragging heavy hose from the barn across the pasture.

In the afternoon, the stall had to be cleared of dirty shavings and manure, and fresh shavings had to be shoveled in. Then the feeding routine had to be repeated every evening. I'd always done the brushing and grooming. That continued as well. After a few weeks of dragging, shoveling, brushing, and grooming, my arms were growing stronger.

As I grabbed the fly spray from the tack room, I noticed Medallion's saddle in the corner. Lifting that heavy thing on the day I had taken my first solo ride had been as impossible as climbing Mt. Everest. The week after Dad left, I decided to try it again. I was only able to raise it one foot off the saddle rack. There was no way I could throw it up on the horse.

Each day after finishing my chores, I practiced lifting the saddle. At school, I was also doing chin-ups and lifting weights to build up my arm muscles. It was a personal challenge for me. I figured once I could raise that saddle up to Medallion's back, I could get back in it and start riding again, the right way, the safe way.

I knew from reading several books about horses, there were lighter English saddles I could have handled easier. But Dad purchased the big western saddle as part of the package deal when he bought Medallion. And he was in the process of teaching me how to do western pleasure riding, trail riding, and possibly, on down the road, barrel racing like they do in rodeos. "We're in Texas for goodness' sake. Why would we want to do English riding anyway?" Dad teased.

During the time I had Medallion, Dad taught me how to lunge the horse to get him ready for a ride. Sometimes I had to keep Medallion trotting, then loping, circling around the corral for twenty to thirty minutes before he would finally settle, calming down enough for us to get a good ride out of him.

After Dad disappeared, I continued the practice of lunging, but that's all I would trust myself to do safely. I could ride bareback in the corral, but it was really uncomfortable riding on the horse's backbone, so a long ride was out of the question. Mom could've raised the saddle up on Medallion for me, but it was all she could do just working every day and keeping the house up. She rarely came over to the barn. So I knew I had to figure out a way to saddle up by myself if I wanted Medallion's training to continue.

After a few months, my arms had grown strong enough to pick the saddle up and lift it over my head. Now I just had to swing it up and over Medallion's back and cinch it in place. It was now time for me to "Cowgirl up." I wasn't too sure how Mom would react to me saddling and riding Medallion by myself, but I figured I'd come this far, and I was determined to see this through. The rest, I'd worry about another day.

"Okay, boy," I whispered to Medallion. "It's been a while since you've worn a saddle. But today is the day." After my regular thirty-minute lunge session in the corral, I brought Medallion back in the barn and tied him to the stall rail. I took a bite out of my afternoon apple and gave the rest to him to eat. It was now my job to get the saddle up and on the horse's back. I must do it with complete confidence, for Medallion was sensitive to my every feeling. It was important to act without fear.

I first got the blanket out of the tack room and walked it up to Medallion, letting him take a nice long whiff of it. When he had figured that thing out, I nestled it on his back and went back to the tack room for the saddle. Easily, I jerked it off the rack and carried it right over to the horse's side.

"Here we go, sweet boy," I whispered. Then I took a deep breath and yanked the heavy leather contraption up onto the loading step. My arms began to quiver. I balanced on the step and lifted the saddle up to shoulder level and over onto the horse's back. It plopped into place, and Medallion tossed his head up and down, nickering his applause. I wiped sweat from my forehead, pleased with my tiny accomplishment, and hopped down to scratch Medallion under his chin.

"We're taking baby steps forward, aren't we, boy? Now all I've got to do is get things moving in a positive direction inside the house, and we will all be just fine." But sadly, inside, there were few forward steps being made.

## One Step Forward, Two Steps Back

After six months or so, Medallion and I were safely riding in the pasture and around our neighborhood. Things were better than ever with him, but my home life was rapidly in decline.

The phone rang as I entered the house. Mom grabbed my arm and pulled me up close to her face. The smell of wine nearly knocked me over. "I need you to answer that. If it's a bill collector, tell them the check's in the mail. They keep leaving messages on the recorder, and they just won't stop calling. It's driving me crazy!"

She stumbled away, and I rolled my eyes behind her back. I hated covering for her. I knew things would probably get tight when Dad left, but I had no idea it would be this quick or this bad. Just as Mom suspected, it was a bill collector calling, this time from the electricity company. "My mom said to tell you the check's in the mail," I lied.

"It better be in the mail and here by Monday, otherwise, the electricity's going to be cut off," the man curtly responded. When I went to relay the message, it set off another round of Mom's waterworks. She walked over to the nightstand and grabbed her package of cigarettes. She had started smoking again after the divorce went through. Flopping down on the edge of the bed, Mom's hands shook as she lit one up to go with her cry.

I wasn't sure how much cigarettes or wine cost, but surely with some cut backs there, we could afford to pay the electricity bill. Still, as she took a long drag, her nerves seem to calm a bit. Maybe now wasn't the best time to pressure her to quit.

If only I could get a job, I could help her with some of the bills. But at ten years old, jobs were hard to come by. I had walked the neighbor's dog a couple of times and did some dusting for them once a week, but the money I earned from that wouldn't even buy a gallon of milk.

I walked over to pat Mom on the back, wiping her hair out of her eyes. "We'll work this all out, Mom. Try not to worry." She grabbed hold of me and gave me one of those nonstop bear hugs she was becoming known for these days. Lately, I felt more like the mother than the daughter. When she seemed to be feeling better, I trudged to my room down the hall to sort things out.

Sitting on the edge of my own bed, I took off my sock, rolling it into a ball. I saw the picture of my dad on my chest of drawers and grew so angry I thought of throwing the sock at the picture. Then I stopped myself, realizing that would be just one more thing I would have to pay for if the frame got broken. So I tossed it at my closet door instead.

If Dad had sent support payments like he was supposed to, things might not have gotten so rough. The last I saw him, he said he was having a hard time too, and this month he would have to put off sending any money. Yes, he had finally showed up about two weeks ago, after his six-month disappearance act.

It seems he'd "found himself" on a business trip to Austin. And in addition to "finding himself," he'd found a couple of other things besides a new girlfriend and her new baby daughter, not his daughter, but one he thought was just "so adorable."

"I can't wait for you to meet them," he said as I walked him back outside to his new Ford Mustang.

"Her car?" I asked, wondering how he could afford all these new things in his life and not be able to afford a lousy support payment for Mom and me.

He answered me with a question of his own, "Isn't she a beauty? We decided to treat ourselves to a new car since we couldn't get away for our engagement. Been great seeing you again, Becky. I'll keep in touch." Then he was off before the words could even set themselves solidly in my brain.

Engagement? Did I hear him right? It had been only six months since he walked out. Now here he was moving to Austin and replacing his old family with a new one like a person might change out a pair of socks. I'd heard of acting before thinking, but this was ridiculous!

I was so furious by the time I rehashed my last meeting with Dad that I balled up the other sock I was holding and threw it at his picture anyway. As it crashed to the floor and shattered into a million pieces, I felt no regrets at all. My dad was beginning to take on a whole other face, one I'd never seen before. And I decided I never wanted to look at it ever again. I picked up the shards of glass and the damaged image of my dad and quickly dumped it all in the trash.

## *Uprooted*

"Finish your packing!" Mom called from the kitchen. "I'm almost done in here."

Sitting in the middle of my room, thinking back to that humiliating tenth birthday two years ago, when my world first started to unravel, I quickly came back to the present when I heard empty beer bottles bursting as Mom tossed them in the trash. My heart twisted in a heavy knot. The sky outside matched my gloom, cold, rainy and blanketed in gray.

I packed the last two things in my backpack: my favorite horse book and a small palomino pony, the perfect size to fit in the palm of my hand. Smoothing down the blond mane with my finger, I whispered, "I wish I could go back to the Christmas Dad gave you to me, when I still believed in dreams."

Looking up where my horse posters use to hang, the walls seemed pale and blank. My bed was packed up and gone. The rocking chair and checkered quilt that Grandma made for my birthday were gone. Of course, Dad was the first one to go. He was long gone, now living his new life with his new daughter.

Everything I had, everything I knew, everything I dreamed of doing was all gone. "I guess it's time for me to go too," I whispered to the pony in my hand.

"Ready, Bec?" Mom poked her head inside the room.

No, I wanted to yell at her. I'm not ready to go. You gave me no choice. No one listened to me anymore even when I had something important to say. They didn't listen, so I wouldn't speak. I just hung my head and fiddled with the zipper on my backpack.

I wished Mom would leave me alone and just go on out to the car, but no, she walked over and stuck out a hand to pull me into her arms. This pretty much sums up my current life, a clingy mom and an empty room.

Staring over her trembling shoulder through the bedroom window, I could see Medallion in the field across the street. He stopped grazing and held his head up, ears perked to attention. Then he swished his tail, sending me a quick farewell.

It broke my heart to think of leaving Medallion in San Antonio, but what really hurt was when I asked Mom about bringing him to Austin and she replied, "It's in your dad's hands. You'll have to talk to him about it."

Like a volleyball, I had been batted back and forth, neither one of them wanting to deal with me.

"Give me one more minute," I told Mom and stiffened in her arms. Reluctantly, she let go, then looked at me with swollen eyes and headed out to the loaded U-Haul.

There was such pressure in my chest, feeling weighted down with anger and guilt. And it was hard staying mad at Mom. She just looked so pitiful all the time.

Surely there was something I could do to fix my family's mess. I was used to fixing things by myself. But no matter how hard my brain searched for answers, the cells fired only blanks. In that moment, amidst the darkness that surrounded me, something became very clear to me. This problem was bigger than me. I had tried to fix things myself and I failed. It was something bigger than I could solve alone. I must somehow now reach beyond myself for the answers. With that flash of clarity, I closed my eyes, bowed my head and prayed, "Please, God …Jesus, I need help."

I had prayed the help prayer hundreds of times but always with the thought that I could fix things myself. This time the prayer was an act of surrendering my pride. I didn't know if things would ever be the same as they once were. But I decided to give my situation to God and trust Him with the outcome. "Trust and Obey," that's the song Grandma sang to me when I was little. Maybe it was time to do just that.

And then, as if in reply to my prayer, fingers of sunlight began slowly stretching across the sky, rising behind Medallion. His coat glistened from raindrops collected on his back. Through the clouds, a shimmering rainbow arched itself from one side of the field to the other growing rich in shades of red, orange, yellow, green, blue, indigo, and violet.

I used my sleeve to wipe off condensation from the window, memorizing every detail of the magical scene. Was it a sign? Ever since that tenth birthday, I stopped looking for signs, stopped hoping for miracles.

But as I watched nature perform, the tenseness in my shoulders relaxed. A peace surrounded me. In that moment I knew, somehow things could change. The dark worry, fear, and dread that had filled me for the last two years were momentarily stilled. I completely gave up the struggle to fix this alone, surrendering my own desires to One Higher, One Smarter, A Power beyond myself. Did I dare begin to hope that all this could work out to be something good? Was this what my former Sunday school teachers called *having faith*?

Outside, Mom gunned the car's engine. I whispered to Medallion, my breath so close it fogged the glass. The golden coat of the palomino became a blur; "Wait for me" was all I could say.

Swiping a single wet drop from my eye, I slung my backpack over my shoulder, turned off the light, and left the darkness behind.

# The Big Move

After Dad left, Mom and I tried sticking it out in San Antonio. But without a college education, the money Mom was able to earn working at Target was barely enough to keep us both fed. Financially and emotionally, Mom was going down fast. When the bank notified her that they would be foreclosing on the house, she swallowed her pride and contacted Grandma and Grandpa in Austin for help.

It was decided we would move there to make a new start. Mom was going to enroll in a junior college to continue her education. And she had already gotten a new job lined up close to our new apartment. Since Dad was there, we both hoped I could go see him more often. Medallion would be staying in San Antonio and looked after by a local vet until Dad could decide whether or not to bring him to Austin.

During the first leg of our move, the car passed through scattered thunder showers. Mom stole sips from a beer can, sniffed, and wiped tears away when she thought I wasn't looking. I thought the best way to leave my past behind and to give Mom some thinking space was to sit in the backseat and get lost in the pictures of my horse book.

I loved looking at all the different colors of horses, forming their own sort of rainbow. However, instead of pastel colors, the horse coats started with dark shades of black, brown, bay, and chestnut and ended with light shades of white, gray, and cream. Then of course, there were the Native American paints that roamed wild through the plains. I liked all the horses.

But the ones that held my heart were the golden palominos. As I flipped through the pages of the book searching for horses that looked like Medallion, a dream of sorts began to form in my mind, more like a prayer really, that one day I would get my horse back, and Dad back, and get on with my life.

I had just dozed off, halfway to Austin near the Outlet Mall in San Marcos, when the sweet dream I was having took a tailspin into a nightmare—a real one! Mom slammed on her brakes, missing the cement road divider by inches. The car, with its tailgating U-Haul swerved, throwing me against the door. My backpack flew to the floor, spilling out its contents.

Thankfully, Mom grabbed the wheel with both hands and held on until she got the car back under control.

"Jeez, Mom, take it easy," I gasped, reaching down to pick up my brush and the little plastic pony. I stared at her red eyes and pale face in the rearview mirror.

On the wheel, her hands shook. "This stupid road construction, it's almost impossible to drive around!" she defended herself. "I need something to calm my nerves."

At the next exit ramp she pulled off and ran into the Quick Stop. When she came out, she took one last swig from a cup of coffee she had bought to sober up from the beer she had drunk before and tossed it in the trash on her way out to the car. "Here ya go, kiddo," she said, tossing a chocolate Easter Bunny into the backseat where I was. "This little treat ought to hold you till we get to Grandma's." As if my snack was the reason for the stop.

Curling up like a snail in a shell, I huddled with a blanket wrapped around my body and nibbled at a chocolate ear. Willing myself not to think about what almost happened, I calmed my nerves by thinking of past Easter celebrations with Dad hiding eggs and Mom sewing dresses for me to wear to church.

Soon, I drifted back off to my nap. The last thirty minutes of the trip I awoke to see the sun burning away most of the rain clouds, and Mom's waterworks finally stopped. She actually seemed to be patching herself together a bit as she fought the Easter traffic into Austin. "Getting hungry?" Mom sniffed and blew her nose one last time.

"I'm always hungry," I had to admit, folding up the blanket and laying it on the seat beside me.

We were just crossing Town Lake in Austin and around the next bend, I could see the Capitol and the University of Texas Tower. Grandpa had taken me on tours of those buildings during one of our visits last summer. He was like a tour guide. "Look here, Becca. Look over there, Becca," he bubbled.

It might be interesting to live near my grandparents. They would surely do all in their power to give history some life.

"Grab my cell and give Grandma a call. She's expecting us and should have some lunch just about ready," Mom said. "Tell her we'll be at the house in about fifteen minutes."

It took six rings to get Grandma to the phone. "I'm up to my eyeballs in flour, young'un. You say you're fifteen away? Well, it's about time you got to Austin. The ham's past done and the bread's burnt, so get on in here. I been awaitin' all morning long, already got three pies made. And keeping Grandpa out of them is about to send me up a wall!"

"Don't climb the wall till I get there, Gran. We'll rock climb together." I had this funny visual cross my mind of Grandma in her apron and knee-high stockings halfway up the rock wall at the Dell Diamond baseball park.

"Rock climb?" she asked, not having a clue what that meant, and missing my little joke altogether.

"See ya soon, Gran. Love ya." I clicked off the cell and gave Mom a lopsided grin. "Gran and I might do a little rock climbing later."

Mom glanced back at me with a puzzled look.

"Grandma sounded a little grumpy as usual, so I was just trying to lighten her up a bit, but she didn't get the joke. It sounds like she's cooking us a feast. Not that I need it," I added, pinching the roll of skin that sat like an inner tube around my tummy.

Since the divorce, I had a hard time keeping my mind on anything constructive. I'd always had perfect grades, but now in middle school, they were really beginning to slip. Ever since that birthday party fiasco, I felt the whole world knew my business, and I hated that. So I sank into this silent world of my own.

Medallion was my only real friend. I'd go out and brush him every afternoon. About once a week, I'd struggle with that heavy saddle, and I'd ride around the pasture. But soon, it got boring just loping around the same place all the time by myself, so I slowed down that activity. As the months wore on, I found myself riding less and less.

Money was tight. We never went anywhere except to the fast-food hangouts around the house. So about all I did was sit in my room, play video games, and eat snacks.

When I got out of my sweats and started dressing for school after winter break last year, I noticed my jeans were getting tight. I really didn't think much about my weight gain until I overheard my old nemesis Sue Ann one day in gym class calling me Becky Butter Belly.

Needless to say, my life had become pretty terrible. So before I realized Medallion wouldn't be joining us, when Mom first got this job offer in Austin, I was actually excited to be moving "to greener pastures." Now, here we were pulling up for lunch at Grandma's, and all I could think of was just how good those pies were sounding to me right about now.

## New Surroundings

"**N**ow don't you two young'uns expect your grandpa to be liftin' a bunch of heavy furniture up them apartment stairs. You know his back ain't that of a spring chicken no more. Pass me them breadsticks," Grandma said as she reached across my face, her flabby arm skin an inch from my nose.

Mom passed the breadbasket to grandma and replied, "Don't worry about Grandpa, Mama. He's coming over just to lend a hand. Tom agreed to meet us over there and help with the heavy stuff."

My heart jumped at the sound of my Dad's name. The last time I saw him was right after Christmas. Since he had moved to Austin with his bride and the new baby girl, it was even harder for him to bring me to his house for visits. Besides, I just figured Dad wanted to focus on his new daughter anyway. Outside the storm clouds circled again and thunder growled in the distance.

Thinking about how Dad had just thrown Mom and me away and moved in with this brand-new family made me feel like throwing something as well. In spite of how bad he had treated us, I still wanted him back in my life. And that made me even madder at myself than at him. "I'll take some more of that macaroni and cheese," I mumbled. Then I grabbed another breadstick to go with the pasta.

"This salad sure tastes yummy," Grandpa invited. "Cowgirls love salad. It helps them sit mighty sweet in the saddle." He leaned over and gave me a quick hug, gently insinuating I needed to watch the carbs. So giving Gramps a reluctant grin, I put back the breadstick and filled up the empty hole on my plate with salad instead.

"Although, I don't really think I'll need to worry about sitting in a saddle anytime soon," I explained to Grandpa. "Dad said we had to leave Medallion behind in San Antonio when we moved out of our house. I don't understand it, and he wouldn't explain it to me. He just said he had plans for him, and then he said, 'Gotta go,' like he always does and that was it."

Clouds came back and covered Grandma and Grandpa's house with a heavy crust of gray. Thunder cracked and rattled the windows. "Well, so much for the backyard egg hunt." I leaned against Grandpa, and he rubbed my shoulder. "Besides, I guess I'm too big anyway." No guessing about it, I knew twelve was too old for egg hunts, tooth fairies, or Santa Claus.

Suddenly I felt tired and had for once lost my appetite. I excused myself and took my backpack to the guest bedroom to be alone with my thoughts. Taking out my little yellow pony, I began stroking its mane and tail with the little toy brush like I used to do when I was three.

Sometimes I wish I could go back there, back to the Christmas when I first got the little yellow pony. The memory of that time was so vivid in my mind…

Dad scooped me up out of bed, the ball on his Santa Claus hat bobbing around his cheek. Logs roasted in the fireplace and filled the living room with a delicious coziness while "Frosty the Snowman" jingled in the background.

"Ho-Ho-Ho," he laughed, cuddling me in his lap under the tree. Mom held a cup of hot chocolate and curled up close to us. For a few quiet moments under the spell of the twinkling white lights and melody of "Silent Night," my family whispered the magic words of the Christmas story and spoke of God's gift of love to His world. Everything was perfect.

Then the excitement began. Dad embodied the joy of Christmas. With a hug, he handed me my stocking. It was full of candies, nuts, and tons of those clear tiny balls filled with toys like those I always begged for as we were leaving the grocery store. After the stockings, it was time for the big stuff.

Dad loved to pull jokes on us. He gave Mom a big box that had a picture of pots and pans on the front. She had been hinting at those for months. But when she opened the box, she was surprised to find a set of old paint cans from the garage. The actual pots were separately wrapped as Mom later discovered in the course of the gift spree.

He had surprises for me too. The first was a ring he had tucked into the shell of a walnut! The grand finale stood waiting at the back of the tree. It was the perfect gift for a daughter who shared her father's love of the golden horse.

In a time when most of my friends' dads grew up dreaming of Star Wars, mine always envisioned himself as a cowboy, his horse of course, the stunning palomino.

Dad's dream became mine as I sat in his lap, and we'd watch the Nick at Night channel on TV. We'd laugh at Mr. Ed, the talking palomino. And we'd cheer as an old cowboy from the '50s named Roy Rogers and his best friend, a palomino named Trigger, rode the Happy Trails.

That Christmas morning, Dad bubbled like a kid as he dragged the huge square box out from behind the tree. It was as tall and wide as my three-year-old self was. I yanked open the paper only to find a smaller box wrapped inside and another and another and another until finally I came to a box about the size of my hands. Inside was the little yellow pony.

As I held it in my hand, I looked into my dad's eyes and saw mirrored there complete love and joy. I think in that moment, my dad must have had the original idea to one day buy me a real palomino.

So many years later, while surfing the Internet, he happened upon "the deal of a lifetime," and I ended up with a stallion…at age eight. Age eight…a turning point in my life when Medallion came into the family and won my heart, the fighting between my parents became known to me, and the magic of my youth slowly began to ebb away.

Shortly after the purchase of Medallion, Mom and Dad began to argue about the horse. Of course that wasn't all they fought about, but it certainly came up often enough.

To hear Mom tell the story, Dad went "clear out of the blue" and bought Medallion. The first thing she told Dad was "A stallion is too much horse for a child. Medallion is too spirited and strong. I'm afraid he's going to hurt Becky."

Dad countered, "But with a stallion as beautiful as Medallion, we might one day be able to have a little Palomino pony, a beautiful one to give our little princess."

Of course that thrilled me! To be considered my daddy's princess and to have a real pony that I could brush and comb and braid its mane, like my little toy pony, why it was all like a magical dream to me!

Mom burst my bubble the minute she rolled her eyes and continued with her second point. "Tom, you're always buying things we don't need without thinking things through." Maybe all this had something to do with what my old teacher Mrs. Lipstick called *cause and effect*. Dad bought Medallion, *the cause*, and my life began to fall apart, *the effect*. At least that's how I was looking at things now; all this divorce thing was bound to be my fault.

As it turned out, Mom was right on both of her points. Not until the morning of my tenth birthday was I even able to begin riding Medallion on my own, and this was done with a considerable amount of danger as I recalled about that full-moon morning.

Mom was right about the cost of Medallion as well, and that was something my dad really should have considered more carefully before purchasing him. Buying a horse was the cheap part. Keeping up with payments on the stable, food, vet bills, saddle, bridle, blankets, and horseshoes grew very expensive.

The cost factor never made sense to me until Mom started sharing with me her concerns about paying the bills and until we lost our house because we couldn't afford it. With all that, I began to realize at least to some degree, the important part money played in my world.

All of this was important of course, but what mattered most right now was the fact that Medallion had become my best friend. And I desperately missed him.

Listening to the rain as it continued to splash against the windows of Grandma's house, I kissed my little pony and sat him on the bedside table, turned out the light, and pulled the blanket up around myself, dozing off to nap in my usual cocoon. As I dozed off, Medallion galloped to greet me. I wiggled free of the blanket and stretched out my arms, flying toward my horse and our dreams.

# New School, New Support

"A support group? Principal Snow suggested I join a support group?" I couldn't believe it. A brand-new school and already the principal recommended me for a support group.

"What's wrong with a support group, Bec?" Mom asked.

"Sometimes, Mom, you are so lame. A support group means I need *support*. It means I can't solve my own stuff, like I got problems or something. I've seen the way it works, kids being pulled out of class to go meet with the counselor. Most of the kids have real problems, like they cuss out a teacher in class or write on the walls in the bathroom. What have I ever done that would make Principal Snow think I need a *support* group?"

Mom looked down at her hands and started rubbing her ring finger, the one that now had no wedding ring. She did that a lot lately when she was worried, and I noticed it every time.

"Well, honey, when we first got to the new school last spring, I talked to your teacher and the principal about some behaviors I'd been noticing and asked them to keep an eye on you to make sure you were okay. After summer break, the principal called to let me know about this special support group that she thought might be just the thing to help you feel better."

"Help me *feel* better? I feel fine! I go to class, I sit quietly in my chair, I talk to no one, what more does she want?"

"That's just it Bec, you are too quiet and too alone. That's not like you, sweetheart. Before the trouble...before your dad and I...split up, you were always talking to one friend or another. You laughed and joked and wore the brightest smile on your face. Now all you want to do is eat and sleep. You hardly ever smile and you seem so angry, mostly at me." Then, yet again, another flood of tears swam down my mother's face.

"You're the one who needs a support group, Mom. You never see anyone either, and you cry all the time," I stormed, stopping myself before I added the one thing I worried about the most.

It was time Mom started going for support because, up until now, all she went for was a bottle and another and another.

Mom got very quiet. She picked up a tissue to wipe her eyes and blow her nose. "You know, hon, I think you're right. That's why you're staying with your dad tonight while I go for some support of my own. The decision is yours. But think about this group, Becky. It starts up next week, and I think some support might do us both some good."

## *Hanging Out with Dad*

Mom dropped me off at Dad's house around six thirty, just in time to make her seven o'clock support group meeting. I never knew whether to knock or just walk right on in. Dad said it was my home too, but I still felt like an intruder.

So I took a deep breath and blew it back out, listening to the baby inside screaming and throwing a tantrum.

Opening the door a crack, I called, "Hello." I wasn't sure if it was loud enough to be heard above the squeal. I was just about to yell out again, but all of a sudden from around the kitchen corner, out raced a white powder puff barking and dancing up and down on his back legs like a miniature bear in the circus.

"Well, well, what have we here?" I cooed and reached down to scoop up the squirming ball of fur. A quick pink tongue popped out and slurped me right across the lips. I snuggled my nose in the soft fur behind the pup's ears and kissed him in return.

"I see you've met your new baby fur brother," Dad said, rushing in and giving me a hug and a zerbert behind my ear.

"Daaaad," I shrieked. "I'm twelve years old, almost a teenager, too big for zerberts."

"You'll never be too old for sloppy, blow-poppy kisses," Dad said, and he tickled me and gave me three more zerberts just for good measure. All the time this was going on, the fur ball was barking and passing kisses from Dad to me and back again.

"Hold it." I giggled and pulled free of Dad's arms. "Let's talk fur ball. Who is this little powder puff? Is he yours?"

"His name is Pooh Bear, and he is not mine," Dad announced.

My face fell. "Well, whose is he?"

"He's ours…yours and mine. I told you, he's your new little fur brother," said Dad. Now trot on into your bedroom, put your stuff away, and take the fur ball with you. I'm going to have a little talk with Kelly about that screaming and then help Marcy pull dinner together."

I put Pooh Bear down on the floor and raced off to my bedroom. I charged into the room, dropped my backpack at the door, and flopped on the bed. Pooh was quick on my heels but stopped with continuous hops at the edge of the bed, his front paws only reaching the bottom six inches of the mattress.

Reaching down, I pulled him into my arms and onto my tummy as my head fell back on the pillow. Like a flash, he skipped up to my face and began covering it with juicy, puppy-breath kisses.

"Pooh Bear," I teased in a baby-like voice.

The puppy stopped its licking, sat on my chest, and cocked his head to one side as if to ask, "What?" His deep chocolate-brown eyes melted my heart like a Snickers on hot cement.

"You are just toooo cute, Pooh Bear. Hmmm…Pooh Bear, kind of a funny name since you look more like a baby polar bear than a Winnie-the-Pooh bear." But he did have some coloring on the tips of his ears about the color of the old stuffed Pooh Bear I used to sleep with. Leave it to Dad to remember that and name him after my old toy.

I knew enough about dogs to know this little fur ball was a Pomeranian. My old friend Irene had invited me over to her house once. She had a Pom, and I had fallen in love with it instantly. Dad remembered that too. Now I had one for my very own! He was a Pom named Pooh. Cute. So tiny too. On Pet Day I could stick him right in my backpack and carry him to school.

Only I couldn't take him to school because school is where I go when I'm with Mom, not Dad. Now, Dad's place was only for Friday nights and every other weekend. My heart suddenly grabbed that familiar weight, but this time, Pooh barked and kissed it away.

# *In Touch with Medallion*

Pooh and I played until the late-night talk show stopped talking on Dad's TV in the living room. Then I put the puppy in his kennel beside my bed and easily drifted off into peaceful dreams.

It was here, during naps and almost every night, where I met my friend. Rattling a feed bucket full of oats, I called to him in my dream, "Medallion."

Just ahead I saw an arrow of gold streak to the top of a hill covered in bluebonnets. Medallion reared up on his back legs, snorted, and neighed a greeting in return. A gust of wind swept Medallion's tail, and it fluttered a wave.

Down the stallion flew straight into my arms. Nuzzling my face, he whinnied a gentle hello.

"Hungry boy?" I whispered, holding oats on my flat outstretched hand. His whiskered muzzle felt spongy soft, and he breathed warm air against my hand as he scooped up the oats with his teeth and tongue.

In an instant, the dream scene flashed ahead. The bucket disappeared and now in my hand was a leather bridle. Medallion and I were racing through a wide green meadow.

I rode bareback without a saddle or blanket…his white mane and my brown mane both flying, a rush of wind on our cheeks. We were free, sleek, both he and me as one, native maiden and her faithful steed.

Flash! Now I stood in the middle of a huge Lego corral with a brush in my hand, combing his flowing corn silk mane, brushing lightly his forelock, the swatch of hair on his forehead between his eyes. I stood on my tiptoes and kissed the star hidden under those wisps of hair. His brown eyes warmed me clear down to my soul. In him, I found a faithful love none other could give me.

As I stood cuddling Medallion's face, I heard a puppy bark at my feet. "Oh, Pooh, are you jealous?" I asked reaching down to gather him up in my arms. But in that instant, the bark got louder and startled me awake.

Struggling to pull myself from sleep, I looked in the crate beside my bed to see Pooh Bear staring at me with his head cocked, and his eyes begging me to release him from his tiny bedtime crate.

A mixed feeling came over me, one of dread to leave the dream of Medallion, one of need to hold the little white puff that was my reality. Pooh whined a tender plea, and the need to free him and face reality took over the dream.

# The Morning After

Pooh's barking had awoken Kelly, and she cried to be set free as well. I held Pooh in the crook of my left elbow and carried him over to Kelly's crib, just steps away from my bed.

I kissed her on the forehead. "You ready to be freed out of your jail too?" I asked the baby, who replied by flashing me a full-faced grin. Kelly then lifted her arms up to me and began jumping on the mattress.

Since my left arm was busy, I picked up Kelly in my right arm and headed to the back porch with my two released prisoners.

I set them both down and pulled open the sliding glass door that led outside to the courtyard. Both prisoners shot out the door, Pooh straight to a spot of grass beside the patio for his morning potty, and Kelly straight for Pooh's leftover dog food.

Before I could get to her, Kelly was already crunching a handful of dog pellets, a frown creasing her forehead in response to the new and not-so-tasty food.

The scene before me was so hilarious I couldn't help but burst out in laughter. Then just as I was going to rush over and pick Kelly up, Marcy stormed outside, knocking my shoulder as she passed.

Swiping the crumbs from Kelly's tongue, the protective evil stepmother yelled, "Why are you laughing while my baby's eating dog food?" Her uncombed hair stood up around her face like Medusa's head of snakes. Before the woman could unleash anymore venom, I turned and plowed back through the sliding glass door, steaming mad and hurt inside, but keeping it hidden from the outside. I wouldn't dare let her get satisfaction from seeing how upset she had made me.

I ran through the kitchen, grabbed three homemade chocolate chip cookies lying out on the counter, and slammed the door to my bedroom. I would hold up there until Mom came back to get me. "Thanks for the great breakfast," I whispered angrily to the closed door and to my stepmother who stood outside it.

In the middle of my bed, I gobbled every crumb. "I didn't mean to let her eat the dog food," I mumbled under my breath. "I was gonna get her, then this creature attacked me from behind and about tore my arm off before I could save the baby."

Just as I was about to secretly sum up my defense, I heard a gentle knock on the door, "Becca," Marcy whispered, "may I come in?"

*Oh sure,* I thought. *Now she wants to come butter me up. Besides, Becky is the name. Only my grandpa gets to call me Becca,*

I ranted in my mind. But on the outside, all I said was a timid, "Yes, ma'am."

Marcy had gone to her room and combed her silky red hair. Now it lay curved on her shoulders. She looked more like a model for a shampoo commercial than a mythological monster. At first I didn't know which was worse, the monster or the model. However, on second thought, the model definitely was worse because next to her I felt like the fat, ugly monster.

"I'm so sorry, sweetheart," Marcy said gently, coming to sit beside me on the bed. "All I could think when I saw my baby was that she might be poisoning herself or something. I had to get to her as quick as I could. I guess I'm just like a mother bear when I see my cubs in trouble. I'm sorry I yelled at you first thing this morning."

She reached over to pull me into her arms, but I just felt sick to my stomach and stiff as the door. Marcy eventually let go, crossed her hands in her lap, and whispered, "Would you like me to make some pancakes and sausage? I know that's your favorite breakfast."

*You don't know my favorite anything*, I thought. All that I replied, however, was "No thanks. I've already had my breakfast. You better go take care of Dad and Kelly. I've got some things to do in here by myself for a while."

"Okay then," Marcy said, searching my eyes. She gently cupped my chin in her hand then quietly closed the door as she left the room.

*Gag*, I thought. *The monster's trying to make me think she likes me. Yeah right, I know better.* I leaned down and grabbed my backpack from the floor. From a hidden side pocket, I took out a package of powdered sugar donuts and ate every single crumb.

Walking over to the computer, I turned on the latest girl beats up girl combat game and acted out my frustrations with the mechanical warriors. After three hours of battling, I found myself needing a bathroom break and feeling a bit hungry.

Quietly, I opened the door and sneaked to the kitchen for a Pringles snack. I spotted Marcy laughing, rolling a ball with Kelly and Pooh in the living room. Evidently, Dad had left since he was nowhere to be found in the house.

*That's great*, I thought. *Dad's gone, yet again. Now when am I gonna talk to him about getting Medallion back?* Disgusted, I plopped back down in front of the computer, shook the mouse to eliminate the calm ocean fish screensaver, and dove back into the all-woman combat zone for an all afternoon workout.

## *Back in School*

"Have you met any new friends yet?" Mom asked as she served me two slices of warm cinnamon toast. I couldn't believe she was actually fixing my breakfast, now here she had to go and spoil it by asking me about school.

I shrugged, ducked my head, and yanked the crust from my bread. How could I explain the kids I'd met so far as the new kid in middle school? Maybe she expected me to throw a party and invite the guy who pushed my face into my locker when I was searching for my math book. Or maybe the model-thin girls in my gym class who sauntered by laughing and grabbing some of my tummy fat as they passed would like an invitation.

I remember, before the Big Fiasco, looking forward to starting back to school. For me, it was a time for fresh school supplies, setting goals, and renewing old friendships. However, since arriving in Austin last spring, I hadn't made any new friends, so there would be no Back to School Welcome Party this year.

I'm sure there were a few nice people at the new school, but it just took too much energy to get to know which ones you could trust and to smile all the time.

By the second week of school in the fall, I could scarcely muster enough energy to get out of bed. Besides carrying in my head the heavyweight title of "Butter Belly Queen of Rocky Trail Middle School," the locker combination was also still giving me fits. And those rotating schedules scared the peedoodlysquat out of me. I kept dreaming I'd lost my schedule and couldn't remember what classes I was supposed to be in.

To top this madness off, for some lamebrain reason, I had agreed to take Mom's advice and join this stupid afternoon support group. Today was my first day.

So after finally surviving the day, I headed to the meeting. Feeling the withered hot dog and fries I had for lunch doing battle in the pit of my stomach, I went in to sit down and did my usual dork routine, accidentally bumping into this guy named Mark.

"Goodness, girl, let me move over and give you some room. You're as big as a horse." *Pow!* The insult hit me like a fist to the face.

I recognized Mark from my gym class. Some boys had been teasing him on the first day of school. He was reaching for the rope swing when this bully laughed at him and said, "He'll never climb the rope with that *girlie* arm."

Mark had been born with one arm smaller than the other one. He could lift things with it, but it lacked the muscle support it was supposed to have. At the time, I didn't think his arm was any big deal; after all, none of us are perfect.

Besides that, I had focused all my attention on his stormy brown eyes. I found them fascinating. I hated the bullies for teasing him and had been ready to jump in and defend him if he ever wanted me to. But now, after his rude remarks, forget the eyes, I just think he's a jerk.

Not bearing to see the smirks these kids surely had on their faces, I glued my attention to the floor, but I heard them laugh. Tears stung my eyes, but I didn't dare let them fall.

Mark's comments refocused in my thoughts, "as big as a horse"—*Really?* Anyone with half a brain knows a horse weighs about twelve hundred pounds. I certainly don't weigh anything near that, at least not yet anyway, I mused, grinning to myself. I was getting pretty good at this inner-mind sarcasm.

Later, I would find out from the adult sponsor John Phillips, this sarcasm, both inner-mind and outer mouth, was something kids did to cope with hurt. I would learn a lot from Mr. Phillips *later*, but right now, when my world was caving in on me, he was just *late*.

"Sorry, guys," Mr. Phillips quickly apologized as he entered the room. "Principal Snow grabbed me just as I was headed this way. You guys know one another?" he asked. But he might as well have been talking to the bookcase because no one answered, least of all, me.

Chancing a glance up, I recognized Elizabeth, a girl who hadn't said a word since her first day in class. "Darth Vaderess" was the nickname given to her by the Star Wars group. Frankly, all that black she wore from head to toe freaked me out, so I had never even made eye contact.

Of course with bangs hanging over her eyes like a veil, that was near impossible anyway. If truth were known, I was afraid of this girl, afraid to allow her, or anyone else for that matter, to learn about the secrets of my home life or get caught up in the emotional baggage I had buried deep in my soul. So I kept my eyes focused down, and my mouth clamped shut.

Certainly Mr. Phillips had no problem talking. He started the meeting by telling the group about himself since no one else wanted to speak. Come to find out he was new at Rocky Trail Middle School too, but he had been holding "group talks" for ten years at schools in Colorado. He was not married and had no kids, which meant to me he had no experience with divorce or kids' problems.

Just when I was about to give up on this guy, he said something that kind of sparked my attention. In addition to this job, he was also a horse trainer. He owned a ranch just a few miles down the road from the school where he trained and boarded horses and taught kids how to ride. Surveying the room behind him, I noticed pictures of horses and some trophies on the bookshelf by the door.

Mr. Phillips said, "If you all are interested, and your parents say it's okay, we could go over for some Saturday field trips to my ranch. Horses and people have a lot in common," he continued. "That's why for me, training horses and being with kids just makes sense."

Thinking about the special connection I shared with Medallion, this actually made sense to me as well. Maybe this guy's got something interesting to say after all. For the first time in months, a flicker of hope sparked.

At that point Mr. Phillips gave us each a spiral notebook. "I'm going to ask one thing of each of you. Please use this notebook to begin creating your own private journal. Each day, write down feelings you are experiencing, events that impress you, questions that cross your minds. Draw pictures if you like. Add stickers or tape in articles or pictures that appeal to you. This book is for your personal reflections. No one will grade it, question it, or read it. This is basically your dialogue with God. Talk to him as if he was your very best friend. It's okay for you to express your anger. He can handle it. But also don't forget to thank him for all the good things he will bring to your attention. As time goes on, you may want to share parts of your journal with me or this group. But that will be totally up to you. Bring the book with you to our meetings. You may hear something that you would like to jot down to reflect on further."

This was all very exciting to me. I enjoyed writing and drawing. This would kind of be my own personal, private scrapbook, a fun project.

At this point I was feeling pretty good about our meeting. But as we all left, Mark just had to whisper one more dig, "Horses, uh, I mean, ladies first," he snickered. His poof of rude hot air, just snuffed my hope spark completely out. I glared at those dark eyes as I passed him on the way through the door and returned to my original assessment of the group...one dark-eyed smart mouth, one Darth Vader look-alike, and me. Great support.

## Real Support

Turns out my group and our sponsor Mr. Phillips gave excellent support. One Saturday near the end of September when the Texas weather promised a cool, crisp morning, John, as he had invited us to call him, opened up his ranch home to us and our parents for our first visit. "You're going to see some beautiful horses," he assured us.

"I've read several books that suggest trying to see things from the horse's point of view when trying to help them through some tough times," John spoke as we walked. "I once took an old, weak horse away from his herd so I could watch him closer. I put him alone in his own pen. He began to kick the fence rails, knock down buckets, kick the trough, generally made all kind of commotion. He didn't want to die in that pen. Even though the horse couldn't speak, he was trying to communicate.

"I know you guys want to communicate too, and you are. You're just not ready to share yourselves with too many words yet. One day, I'm hopeful you'll be ready to share your feelings.

It makes getting to know the real you a lot easier. But right now, let me show y'all some horse talk."

John introduced us to various horses all over his ranch. Some were in pastures, some were in corrals, and some were isolated in stalls.

After looking at some especially troubled, battered horses, Mark quipped in typical sarcastic form, "I thought you said we were going to see some *beautiful* horses."

"They are beautiful…beyond the hurt," John quietly answered. "Let me show you one that has weathered the storm and come out on the other side." That's when we first met Midnight.

Elizabeth cleared her throat, preparing to speak. We all looked at her in disbelief. This was the first time anyone was to hear a peep from her since the beginning of the year.

"He looks just like Black Beauty from a book my grandmother used to read to me," she whispered, strolling over to his pen. The shiny horse snorted and pranced to her outstretched hand, ears perked, tail flashing hello. His nostrils flared as he blew warm air against her palm and grew accustomed to her scent.

"Let me show you a before and after shot," John said as he pulled two pictures from his wallet.

We could not believe it. In the first picture a dull brown horse with only a hint of black in his coat stood hunched in a muddy, grass-free pen, the size of a normal backyard. His mane and tail were matted and caked with the mud he lived in. Ribs of the horse were clearly outlined, and it was obvious he had nearly been starved to death.

"This same horse, beyond the hurt," John said, laying the second picture over the first. The change was miraculous. In this picture, Midnight, the stunning black beauty that Elizabeth now patted, had a wreath of flowers around his neck, and John stood beside the horse with a trophy in his hand.

"Midnight won 'best of show' five years after that first picture was taken. During that time, a lot of people invested a lot of love in that horse. We began feeding him all the right foods on a regular basis. Every day many of the ranch hands and I looked in on him, brushed him, talked gently to him, loved him faithfully.

"I had him brought here to this corral today so you could meet him, but normally, he runs free on the ranch with his own herd, a loving herd that sticks close by him and lives together near him in peace.

"Midnight's transformation took time and hard work for all of us. But we took it slow and never gave up hope."

Before we left the pen that day, Elizabeth moved the veil of hair away from her eyes. And then she reached up and smoothed the hair between Midnight's eyes and kissed the black beauty on his nose. In that moment, I sensed a spark of hope in Elizabeth that I had never before dreamed possible.

As she turned to face me, we exchanged a smile, and I felt strangely warm inside as we strolled to our cars, almost like friends. She was thinking of Midnight, and I was thinking about Medallion, both of us quiet and reflective but walking together, side by side.

## *Joining the Herd*

After that first visit to the ranch, we began to talk more and John talked less, allowing us to sort through our problems and discover solutions for ourselves. Unlike our teachers who had objectives we had to cover, John simply allowed our topics to surface on their own. Sometimes he suggested that we discuss things we had recorded in our journals.

Another thing he did to help us get started was to lay out a variety of pictures on the table. Someone would generally start talking about one of the pictures and then the discussion proceeded from there.

A picture that generated quite a bit of discussion showed a typical day in a middle school lunchroom. All the groups were seated and appeared comfortable talking and laughing together.

As usual, Mark jumped right in, "This must be a fairy tale lunchroom. Sure not like ours here."

"How so?" John asked.

"There's no one sitting alone," Elizabeth softly replied.

I had to agree. "Yeah, that's where I usually end up…at the invisible table, just me and my invisible friends on both sides."

"Has it always been that way, Becky?" John asked.

Thinking back, even before the River Walk fiasco, I had to admit, making friends had always been a bit tricky for me. Hoping to find some answers, I summoned up the courage to speak honestly with the group, "Secretly, I wanted to be popular, so I'd try joining members of their group whenever they would let me in. But no one really ever talked to me about things that were important to me. Oh, they'd look at me and laugh when I told a joke on myself, but they never seemed really interested in what I had to say.

"Other times, I'd seek out kids like Irene because I felt sorry for them. Assuming they were lower on the popularity ladder than I was, made me feel more comfortable with them." Just hearing myself say that, I suddenly realized I was no better since I was ranking them just like the populars had ranked me.

"Truth is," I admitted, "I don't like all these school groups we have. I never could figure out to what group I belong. I'm still trying to find a place where I can honestly be myself and feel…well, loved."

"At least, you probably feel loved at home," Elizabeth remarked. "I don't even get that feeling there. It's like you said, I'm invisible."

Mark chimed in as well, "Right on, sisters. Invisible is the word. Since my folks split, even before that really, it's been all

about them. I keep wanting to know...*where's the love man?*"
We all laughed but secretly shared his pain.

"It sounds like you all are a bit tired of being invisible.
Why not try becoming leaders?" John asked.

"You're kidding, right?" Mark laughed. "I'd just like to be
included in the human race, forget being a *leader.*"

"Are there groups and leaders in the animal world?"
Elizabeth whispered.

"That question sounds like one posed by a *peaceful
leader* and the perfect one to pursue and discuss at our next
ranch meeting," John remarked calmly. "Are you all free
this Saturday?"

## *Peaceful Leaders*

"Let's look in on the horse cafeteria. Maybe we can get some hints from nature on how effective leaders work," John suggested.

We'd arrived just as John's ranch hands doled out grain in the iron food troughs. There were about fifty horses in the pasture and ten feeding stations.

"There's one important thing you have to remember about the animal kingdom. Their sole purpose in life is to remain alive from one day to the next," continued John.

From my perspective, that's about where I was too, just trying to survive, one day at a time. Eating was a big part of survival, of course, and it was interesting to see how the horses went about it.

There appeared to be two different kinds of groups, the bosses and the peacemakers.

The bosses, led by a feisty red gelding, stormed over to the ranch hands and began butting the feeding cans with their heads. They stomped their feet and pushed and shoved to get around the first two troughs that were filled. As other horses filtered in close for their share, the nipping and rudeness continued.

Interestingly, the majority of horses stood back and waited. After the first few began eating their fill, this older buckskin sauntered up to a trough on the side where the less aggressive horses were and calmly began nibbling the grain. The rest of the horses walked over; the buckskin politely moved over, and all joined right in.

During the feeding, while the bosses continued nickering, pawing the dirt, and fussing with each other, the buckskin and his larger group finished their meal in peace.

"That red horse reminds me of a certain Barbie doll I once knew in San Antonio," I recalled with a shudder. "She and her two sidekicks were always vying for power. I wanted to be with them, but I never really fit in," I had to admit.

Mark noticed the buckskin. "What's the story on that horse?" he asked. "It looks like he's kind of a leader too, only in a peaceful way."

"That's what I noticed too," John agreed. "The other horses seem to respect him in a different way. He's still their leader, but he's more of a buddy, so that's what I named him. Remember what I told you earlier, it's all about survival. The Buddys of the world may have learned the secret. They can still be leaders, but they've chosen to lead with a certain respectful confidence."

"And peace," Elizabeth quietly joined in.

John gave her a warm smile. She beamed right back at him. And we all began to sense and take ownership of the kind of leadership we had learned from watching Buddy.

# The Ranch Community

By Christmas, Rocky Trail Middle School was running like a well-practiced computer video game. Everyone knew everyone else, and most worked and played together as a family. This was due in no small part to the bond between Principal Snow and John.

Turns out they both loved animals and knew how important the creatures were to children. They set out to build a sense of the ranch community and filled the school with their ideas.

"Animals are gifts from God," John always said. "He gave them to us from the very beginning of time, to have dominion over them, but also to help us. Think about it, there are animals all over the world, in every environment. So no matter where people are, animals are there too. Not only are they here for us to love, but they can also love us…unconditionally." I thought of little Pooh Bear and Medallion when John said that.

"God made animals to teach us other things too. Even tiny ants have many lessons for us to learn." For that reason, John always had plenty of animals around.

At the beginning of the school year, he brought up several fish aquariums for the counselor's room and the cafeteria. All along the walls at the front of the school, Principal Snow let him set up other aquariums that could be checked out to the classrooms. They were filled with snakes of all kinds, turtles, and iguanas. Hedgehogs and guinea pigs were class favorites. Teachers especially liked their quiet, calming natures.

A small family of rabbits hopped around the library and sat in student's laps as they read and did research projects.

Parent involvement with a no-tolerance policy toward bullies was established as a strong focus at the school, and the unique practice of observing and caring for animals everywhere helped create within the school a unique atmosphere of cooperation and peace.

In my personal life, peace became more prevalent as well. All during the fall semester Mark, Elizabeth, and I worked together, making discoveries about our families, our situations, and ourselves.

Our last official meeting as a "support family" took place at the ranch where we met the yearlings, and John talked to us about how we were like them, growing up and learning to take responsibility for our own actions. He challenged us to take the focus off our parents and to concentrate on becoming the peaceful leaders we were born to be.

John took the role of an even more passive leader, always available for us if we needed him but never pushy or overly preachy.

Eventually, he released us from meeting as a group. That was a little sad, but freeing, too, knowing that he trusted us enough to let us step out on our own. He set us up as his school ranch hands, putting us in charge of gathering up other ranch hands to help feed and care for the animals at the school.

Mark had the idea of setting up a place in the school for some of John's unique animals, like the piglet born with only three legs, a blind hamster, and the parakeet with a broken wing. His confidence and self-esteem soared as he organized a group of kids to work with these special animals. Most of the members became so interested in the science of zoology they considered later going into veterinary training.

Elizabeth and I started a club known as the "Helping Hands" where we all met frequently after school to discuss ways to support students not only in our school but also in the community. This group established tutoring sessions, held new-student welcoming activities, and set up committees to work with Habitat for Humanity to help build homes in our neighborhood.

John's ranch became an extension of the school campus. Parents were also included in our school's community-building efforts. They hauled hay bales from the ranch to build scarecrows for our fall festival. We had so much fun working weekends in October at the pumpkin patch. Monies earned there went to the Salvation Army for their winter coat drive.

In November, John offered classes about turkeys and chickens. He even had bulletin boards set up to show the different kinds of birds found in and around Texas, and of course, we had a traditional Thanksgiving feast at the ranch.

December, however, brought the grandest event of all. Mark, Elizabeth, and I went to John with the idea of having an old-fashioned country Christmas at his ranch. He agreed, but only with the understanding that we would help with the planning and decorating.

Before the first guests started to arrive, Elizabeth grabbed my hand, and we ran through the barn to make sure everything was in place. John had cleared out all the animals. We covered the floor with sweet fragrant sawdust, then decked out the rafters with boughs of cedar, pine cones, and red berries.

In the center of the barn stood a ten-foot tall blue spruce Christmas tree all decorated with red balls, strings of popcorn, and handmade cowboy ornaments. Mark plugged it in, and the tree burst forth with hundreds of tiny white lights.

Seeing it all lit up that night for the first time, Elizabeth shouted, "That's the most beautiful tree I've ever seen!"

At the base of the tree, John knelt down and tucked a small object into the cotton snow. It was a cowboy Santa with boots on, a cowboy hat held in his hand, bending down on one knee in front of Baby Jesus in the manger. I glanced over at Mark wondering if I was the only one who noticed the resemblance of the cowboy Santa to John. He noticed the similarity as well and winked at me in agreement.

Families started piling in, all bringing food to share, and placed it out on long tables decorated with checkered table-cloths. There were turkeys, hams, and plenty of fried chicken, corn on the cob, and green salads. Desserts too so that everyone had at least three different kinds to choose from. Music and laughter exploded off the walls of the decorated barn.

After the feast, guests huddled in horse-drawn wagons filled with hay. We rumbled past neatly kept pens where potbellied pigs rooted and played with rubber soccer balls. Peacocks strutted in the yard and yelled out from the oak trees. We passed dairy cows mooing and chewing cud. Mark piped up, "Did you know cow's cud is barfed up grass?"

"Thanks for sharing," I rolled my eyes and looked over at Elizabeth. She smiled back. Her grin sparkled like the stars above us. The hayride stopped in a field where a warm Yule log sent up circles of smoke and fiery popping sparks.

Families circled and sang Christmas carols and cowboy songs the choir teacher had taught us. Then as a treat, we sipped on cups of hot chocolate, which parents poured for us from steaming thermoses.

In the warmth of the fire, the community grew close and united in spirit. As we all filtered away to begin the winter holiday, families carried with them love and support like we had never known.

Mark, Elizabeth, and I stood next to John as the final guests were pulling away. "What you did tonight, bringing us all together, it was really cool, man." Mark extended his hand to John for a warm handshake.

"Twern't me, Magee, it was the best idea *you all* have had yet." John laughed. Mark blushed in reply, then quickly jogged off to unplug the Christmas tree.

Giggling, Elizabeth and I hugged like the best of friends. Little bells jingled from Elizabeth's ears. John had been so busy, he hadn't even realized till then, but Elizabeth was no longer dressed in black. She wore a red sweatshirt with a green elf on the front. "Don't you look bright and cheery, my dear." John smiled.

"I've never seen so many happy families as there were tonight," Elizabeth shyly whispered. "My mom and dad are letting me spend the night with Becky. And guess what... they were holding hands when they left. They said to tell you they had a great time."

My mom had been clearing away the last of the food when she joined the group. I pulled her into my circle of friends and said, "Mom, thanks for getting me to join this group. I'm beginning to feel like a real person again."

This statement seemed to move John the most, and he looked down at his boots to keep the group from seeing his flood of emotion. He cleared his throat, tipped his hat with a wink at Mom, and stated, "Well, folks, it's been real nice having everyone here tonight. I better get in and hit the bunk. I've got a few horses to shoe come sunup. By the way, thanks you guys for making me feel so welcome in your community. You young people have become real leaders."

Mark, Elizabeth, and I piled into the backseat of my mom's car. We realized as we left that night something truly special, a real miracle had happened in each of our lives, for we not only had become leaders but also the dearest of friends.

# Trouble Back in San Antonio

A gentle spirit followed us into the New Year and sped the months along. It was already March before some disturbing winds blew through my way.

"Hi, Dad!" I bubbled as I ran to pick up the phone. "Guess what, I lost five more pounds! By the way, it's good to talk to you. You never call during the week. What's up?"

"Becky," Dad hesitated, "I have some terrible news. I hate to tell you this over the phone...but Medallion was in an accident."

The tone in Dad's voice left my chest tightening in fear. "Dad, is he dead?" I whispered.

"No, sweetheart, he's not dead, but...he was hit by a car, and he's not doing well."

"Hit by a car? But he's in a pasture. What happened, did a drunk driver go through the pasture?"

"No, the fence on the side by Ingram Road, well, it was getting weak. Evidently, Medallion had been pressing on it, trying to get to a patch of green grass on the other side. He knocked down a post and..." Dad's voice broke. I could hear him struggling to regain composure. "Medallion got out in the street. A car came over the hill and ran into his side."

Stunned, I felt like someone had just shoved a fist into my gut.

"Becky," Dad said gently, "sweetheart, are you okay?"

I swallowed hard, blinked back tears, and tried to find words to continue. "What now, Dad? What happens now?"

This conversation was getting harder and harder for Dad. "The vet says we should put him down."

"Put him down? You want to *murder* him?" I yelled into the phone.

"Honey, this isn't murder, it's relief. Medallion is almost physically healed except for some surface wounds on his face and side. But something has happened to him. He was spirited before, but he's really taken a nosedive. Now he acts crazy."

"Crazy? This whole thing is crazy," I cried. "You said he's physically healed! When did all this happen? Why are you just now telling me all this?"

"It happened that weekend you came for a visit, right after school started back, in September. Remember when you woke up at the house and I was gone? That's where I was. I asked Marcy to tell you I was on business. When I heard about the accident, I rushed over to San Antonio to check it out. Doc and I have been in touch ever since. I wanted to make sure Medallion was healed so you didn't have to see him all messed up. You're so young. I just didn't want to upset you needlessly. I'm so sorry, baby."

I couldn't believe it. Medallion lay hurting for months, both Christmas and Valentine's Day had passed and still Dad hadn't even shared this terrible news with me. Just when I thought I could trust him, and my relationship with my parents had begun to heal, now this.

Anger, deathly fierce, began churning in the pit of my stomach, a volcano about to blow. Then I remembered John's words during one of our sessions, "Share your feelings... masking them inside only makes the anger worse. Find the words to tell the person who is hurting you."

I took a deep breath and slowly let it out, relaxing my shoulders. "Dad, I'm not a baby. I can hear sad things. I feel you weren't being honest with me. You kept this terrible news from me for months. I feel so mad at you right now!" Trembling, I stood with my feet planted to the ground. We were like two angry dogs, facing off for battle.

But the words were out. I told Dad exactly how I felt. No matter what he did with the information, at least now he had it, and as John predicted, the pressure valve of anger correctly opened and some of the hurt slowly fizzed out.

"Dad, I want to see Medallion. You must take me there before anything else is decided. Medallion is my horse. You bought him for me. I need to be in on the decisions about him from now on." I took another deep breath, then added, "One more thing, I want my friend John Phillips to come with us when we go to San Antonio."

"Your support counselor, John Phillips?" Dad asked.

"Yes, Dad. John Phillips is my counselor, but he is also a horse trainer. He helps horses exactly like Medallion that are hurting beyond the scars. And Dad...John Phillips is someone I can trust."

A full thirty seconds passed before Dad made a sound. "Well, it sounds like your mind is made up. I'll pick you and your Mr. Phillips up at the school around eight Saturday morning...if that's all right with you."

"I'll check with John and let you know if that's a problem, but I'm sure it won't be. I know I can count on *him*."

Dad sat paralyzed on the other end of the line. He had never heard me speak so directly to him before.

As I hung up the phone, I wasn't sure how my dad would handle my newly acquired assertion, but at least I didn't pack in my feelings like I always did before.

This news was hard for me to hear, but I had listened, listened to the terrible news about my horse and listened to my dad and all his excuses. When the anger inside me began to rise, I *respectfully* spoke my mind. Big change for me.

Suddenly, remembering something Mom once said to me after one of her support meetings, I repeated the words to myself, "I might not like the situation I find myself in, but I have to like myself in it." So far, I did.

Now it was time to stop rehashing the details of the conversation, thinking only about myself. It was time to turn my attention to Medallion. Right now, he needed my prayers.

# *Help on the Way*

The sun was waking up the morning sky when John and I approached Dad's truck. I introduced the two men, "Dad, this is Mr. Phillips."

Extending his hand for a shake, Mr. Phillips spoke first, "Call me John."

Dad's cowboy hat tipped as he nodded to the counselor, "Tom Harris," his voice clipped. Both men stood eye to eye and firmly shook hands.

Before he had even exited the parking lot, Dad quizzed John, "So what makes a middle school counselor an expert on damaged horses?"

I cringed and stared at Dad in horror. *Damaged*, I thought; it sounded like he was talking about a broken computer instead of a living, loving creature.

John cleared his throat, "I'm no expert by any means, but I've been working with horses since I turned ten, raised on a ranch just outside of Denver. As an adult, I started training horses and took a special liking to ones that had problems.

"After moving here to Austin, I bought a ranch about five miles away from Rocky Trail and now in addition to working with children. I work with horses whose owners contact me about resolving training problems.

"Occasionally, I buy ones that people have given up on." Then he turned and looked Dad straight in the eye. "I'm not accustomed to giving up on animals or people."

"Good enough," Dad answered quietly. Then he and John talked about Medallion for the first hour of the trip.

Conversation between the two men grew easy and tension free. But as I sat in the backseat like a scared helpless rabbit, staring at my dad's curly black locks, I felt my anger at him rising again.

Sticking my foot underneath Dad's truck seat I kicked him right square in the bottom…Ah, a tiny release, like letting the fizz out of a Coke. He spun around and gawked at me like he couldn't believe I just did that.

"Sorry, Dad, I guess my foot slipped," I lied.

Immediately I felt ashamed of my immature action and the lie, and I wondered, *What have I learned during counseling that could help me curb this anger?*

*Stop and think.*

The words came to my mind, and I bowed my head to ask for forgiveness and the help of God, my Higher Power.

Hoping music would help, as well to calm my nerves, I took headphones out of my backpack and climbed into my own thoughts.

Why did life always hit me like this? Just when things seemed to be shaping up a little...

Mom desperately wanted to start a new life. With Grandma and Grandpa's encouragement, Mom started back to church. She joined an Alcoholics Anonymous support group and made some great new friends. One day at a time she had been able to stop drinking and wasn't crying every second like she used to do. I had real hope that she might be able to break her habit.

She started taking better care of herself in other ways too, dressing nicer and wearing makeup again. Over the last two years, Mom also had put on too much weight just like me, so she began cooking healthier, and we were both going to the gym to work out at least three times a week.

My favorite activity, "walk and talk," occurred almost every night; and we had begun getting back to the mother-daughter fun we shared before the divorce.

Visits to Dad's house improved too. On warm winter days, he took Kelly, Pooh, and me to the park. He set up a basketball net, and I beat him at "Horse" almost every time we played. Even Marcy, the evil stepmother, didn't seem so bad anymore. She was teaching me how to sew. And on my weekend visits, she had waiting on my bed, current teen magazines. So we used them to try out the latest movie star styles and hairdos.

Elizabeth had become my best friend. This all started around Halloween when she came over and helped me hand out candy to the trick-or-treaters. We fixed her hair, and she tried on one of my old princess costumes. She had such a blast dressing up in flashy colors that she did a reverse and now dresses like a rainbow. Of course, the thing that helped the most was that *Darth Vaderess* and I had connected on a spiritual level. Now neither of us feels invisible. We don't look down on each other but rather eye to eye and heart to heart like good friends should.

Mark also turned out to be quite a surprise. Once our support group started sharing personal interests and feelings, he actually apologized for saying I was as "big as a horse" during that first group meeting. Then, I found out how much he really loves horses.

For Valentine's Day last month, he sent me a huge card, and even gave me a stuffed pony for my bed, a palomino with a red bow. I smiled, thinking as spring break approached that it would be great to bring Mark to San Antonio to meet my real palomino.

Then reality slammed me…almost as hard as the car that slammed into Medallion. Things had been going so well. Now, here I was on my way to San Antonio, trying to prevent my dad from putting Medallion down.

I should still be furious with my father. How could he even begin to consider killing my horse? But then, I reasoned, holding on to the anger will only hurt my chances of convincing him to save Medallion, and more importantly, it will rob me of any peace I might find today.

By taking the time to stop, think, and thank God for all the progress my family and I had made, my anger had subsided at least for the moment. And I was determined to maintain this level of patience that had come into my heart, no matter how hard my pride fought to be heard.

Respectfully, I broke into the men's conversation, "Are we almost there?"

"Almost, hon, just hang on about ten more minutes," Dad answered tenderly.

Hang on. What more could I do? Nothing more, except to "let go and let God,"[1] praying somehow He could work some good out of what I could see only as hopeless.

# Put Him Down

Slipping off my headphones, I climbed out of the backseat and realized we had not gone to Medallion's old stable. A dark, heavy cloud hovered over an old farmhouse and several corrals lined with a maze of white fences. "Where are we?" I asked, the wind whipping a strand of hair across my face.

"This is Doc Simpson's home," Dad answered as we walked to the barns behind the house. "He's the vet who's been taking care of Medallion for us."

"Howdy," the man called as we entered the main corral. "Best leave the little lady outside for a bit," said the Doc. "We'll take a look first, see how the old boy's doing today."

"Wait outside! No way! I didn't come all this way to wait outside," I stated stubbornly. Thunder rumbled in the distance as tears stung the back of my eyes.

Dad came over, put his arm around my shoulder, and looked me straight in the eye. "Sweetheart, I haven't seen Medallion since the accident. But then, he looked…Well, he looked bad. I really think Doc is right. Let John and me take a quick look, then we'll probably bring you in. Go check out

Doc's new colt over there in that stable around the corner. We'll be back for you in just a minute or two." Then he turned and, without further words, headed toward Medallion's stall.

"Probably bring me in," I mumbled, kicking dirt as I rounded the corner.

Then I spotted him, a tiny black colt wobbled toward me on newborn legs. "You look like a miniature Midnight," I cooed, entering the gate and kneeling down to let the baby lick my outstretched hand.

Midnight, that stunning horse that John had been working with for the last five years, once had problems too. But he had been nursed back to life, and John had decided to keep him around as a good ride for people who came to visit the ranch.

Suddenly, an idea came to me. Since Dad could no longer afford to keep Medallion, maybe John could buy Medallion and take him back to his ranch. Even though he would no longer be mine, at least this way Medallion could be close enough that I could go see him as often as I wanted. Besides, I knew John could help Medallion, just like he had helped me. I gave the colt one final pat on his tiny soft muzzle and then raced around the corner toward Medallion's stall.

John caught me in his arms just as I entered the shaded dark corral near the barn where Medallion was being held. "Whoa there, sweetie," he said gently, kneeling down on one knee.

"John, I just had the best idea!" My eyes looked down at him, wide with hope. "You could buy Medallion and fix him, then you could keep him at your ranch for me—er...uh...for *others* to ride just like you did with Midnight!"

John lowered his eyes and slowly drew random circles in the dust with his finger. Then he looked back up and straight into my eyes. I knew what he was about to say would be honest, even if it hurt. "Becky, I'm not sure I can help Medallion. He's in a pretty bad way. Remember, not everything can be fixed. Some things, we just have to accept. Let go and let God."[2]

Lightning ran across the sky, and the thunder crackled overhead. And in that instant, John tumbled from the pedestal where I had placed him. I wasn't ready to let go of *anything*, least of all Medallion. "I thought you said you never give up on anyone!" I accused.

"I told your dad I'm not *accustomed* to giving up on anyone," John answered. "But there are exceptions, Becky. I can't work miracles."

Gritting my teeth, I just stared at him. My heart pounded, and tears grew full in my eyes. John stood and tried to pull me into his arms, but I jerked away from him and stomped toward Medallion's barn. "I'm going to see my horse," I stated emphatically.

Dad met me at the door of the stable. He could tell I was angry, but he quickly grabbed hold of my shoulders and tilted my eyes up to his. "Becky, most of the original scars have scabbed over, but he's got some fresh new gashes on his chest. It's going to be hard for you to see."

"*New* gashes?" I whispered, looking at him with questions in my eyes.

"I fixed him up from the accident," the old country doctor broke in. "But now he's battling a mind game. One day, he'll be acting normal, grazing and running around in the corral. Then just like he done a minute ago, somethin' sets him off and he just goes plum crazy and starts slamming hisself into fences and knocking against the sides of the stall. It's killin' me to keep doctorin' this horse then watchin' him beat hisself up the very next day.

"Your dad's done paid out thousands of dollars on this horse. Money don't grow on trees, young'un. Medallion's done drove hisself crazy. Ain't no psycho-counselor gonna be able to fix him. You need to put him down." Then the bald-headed ogre marched to his house and slammed the back screen door.

Forcing adult determination into my voice, I stared straight into Dad's eyes and said, "I'm not a baby, Dad. Please let me see my horse…now."

Dad finally gave in and stood aside, motioning me to go ahead of him and John. The thunder rumbled and the shadows deepened as I walked through the barn door and down the hallway toward the back of the barn.

My father and John allowed me all the time I needed to come to grips with the nightmare before me.

After seeing Medallion in this terrible condition, I realized some serious decisions had to be made—adult decisions that I didn't know how to make.

Leaving Medallion in San Antonio those many months ago had hurt beyond belief. But miraculously, I had found ways to go on living. Now the fear of losing my horse forever terrified me, and I wasn't sure if I could go on without him.

As the rain began to drain the clouds, I shuddered, feeling more alone than I had in months…

The thing of it was, however, I was not alone. Before I tumbled down into the pit of hopelessness and depression, I stopped to think. Now I had adults in my life I could trust. I had friends who I loved and who loved me that I could call.

But most important, I had God, who had helped me before and would help me again, walking with me through these frightening storms.

Even if all the people in my life failed me, I now knew I could trust in God alone. For I had learned, beyond a shadow of a doubt, He is faithful. He will not leave me. And He will work all things out for my good, even if I couldn't begin to imagine how.

I remembered when we first moved to Austin, I had shared with my grandma the story of the magical rainbow that I had seen the day I left Medallion in San Antonio. "Something seemed to change in me that day," I told her. "I remembered feeling totally powerless over my life. I was tired of trying to fix things by myself and I called out to God. I remembered just saying, 'Jesus, I need help.'"

"That must have been the moment!" Grandma had exclaimed. "Jesus heard you call his name. He was ready to give you the gift."

"The gift?" I asked.

"Yes, my child. His gift of salvation. He is always ready and willing to give it to anyone who asks for it, anyone who lets go of their pride in running their own life, anyone who admits they are powerless and need help to save them. We have to acknowledge that he exists before he can save us. But just as soon as we do, it's a done deal. Our sins are forgiven—

past, present, and future ones—and Jesus becomes our Lord and Savior. God fills us with his Holy Spirit to guide us that precious Spirit of love, joy and peace."

"Peace...I remember feeling that when I saw the rainbow. It was a peace I couldn't quite understand," Becky whispered. "I could just feel everything would turn out okay. God would be with me, helping me through things."

"But Grandma, I didn't keep feeling the peace. Or the joy, or the love for that matter," I had admitted. "And unfortunately, I still make mistakes and sin, even when I don't really want to do that."

My grandma had shared all these things with me when she introduced me to Jesus a few months ago, and I asked Him to become my Lord and Savior.

She explained that we all sin and that bad things would still happen to us in this life. That is just part of living in this fallen world full of sin. "But don't forget, we also have the gift of God's Holy Spirit to live in our hearts and stay with us when bad times come upon us. His Spirit has sealed us, and it will stay with us forever. His Spirit can help us understand the Bible when we read it. And it is seen in nature and in acts of love that we take time to give and recognize in others." Remembering all Grandma had shared with me, I thanked God for his faithfulness.

Just then, Dad walked over to me and I snapped back to the present. He pulled me into his arms and held me close, letting me cry on his shoulder. I felt this had to be an act of grace, one of those amazing acts of God's love.

# Down and Out

I felt so dizzy and sick at my stomach when we first got back in the truck to go home, I lay down in the backseat and cried myself to sleep. It wasn't a restful sleep though. Unconsciously, as I listened to snippets of my dad's and John's conversation, their words formed nightmares in my mind.

"Repetitive injuries…mind games…healing doubtful… got to put him down…"

My hand, blood dripping over the fingers, grasped the deadly rifle, like the one from the old TV movie *Old Yeller*. It was aimed at Medallion's head. Smoke from the barrel blurred my vision. Then my chest jerked and spun as I held on to his battered body, and we twisted to the top of Dorothy's tornado heading toward the land of Oz to make one last hopeful plea.

"Bec," Dad said gently. He had pulled to a stop in front of a McDonalds just outside of Austin. "Want to grab some supper?" I was glad to have been shaken out of my nightmares, but now I had to face the horrific reality.

I stopped dragging the fork through my salad, looking from Dad to John and asked, "Is there any hope?"

Both men grimly glanced at each other, then back at me. "John, did you talk to Dad about my plan?"

"Yes, we spoke about me buying Medallion," John answered quietly.

"Hon, the trouble is…" Dad cleared his throat and attempted to continue. "We don't know if Medallion could even survive the trip to Austin. We'd have to get him loaded in the trailer for one thing, and that could take a miracle in itself. I think we all need to think and talk this thing over a bit more, then we'll see what happens."

Funny, Dad actually wanted to think things over before acting. Now it was my turn to barge on, "Talk things over? Time is wasting, Dad. That lamebrain Dr. Simpson will probably just let him die while we sit and talk things over," I reasoned. "We've got to bring him home!"

"I tend to agree with Becky on this point," said John. "Timing is crucial when depression's involved. We will need to make some fairly quick decisions before the trauma affects him beyond repair. Trouble is I'm not sure if I'm your man. I've had some troubled horses, but frankly, Medallion's case is the worst I've ever seen." He hesitated and swirled his fork in his own salad. "There are some serious considerations that have to be made."

"We best get going," said Dad as he stood to toss his leftover food in the bin. That was like the old Dad, when the going got tough, he got going. But whatever he chose to do was not something I had control over. I only had control of my own actions.

I decided not to run away and hide within myself but rather to go to friends I knew I could trust for further support. So later that night when we finally got home, I called my friends over, and as we sat on my bed, I explained things to Mark and Elizabeth.

They supported me the best way they knew how, by recalling how John had helped the troubled horses from his ranch, and reminding me of the reassuring, hope-giving phrases he had taught us to recite during difficult times.

It was no surprise that the former "Darth Vaderess" remembered the story of Midnight. "His coat shone like Black Beauty," Elizabeth recalled. "But that wasn't the way John found him. The owner had just about starved the poor horse to death. Remember how John said Midnight just ran and ran around the corral? He turned that big boy around," her friend offered.

"Yeah," Mark added. "Also, remember Tonto, the paint with the crooked ear that John keeps in the back pasture. He's training him to load and unload in the trailer. That was after the horse was in that accident where the trailer came unhitched and somersaulted in the ditch. John got him taking riders again and just about has him back trailer loading. Tonto gave me a great ride the last time I was out there."

I looked into his face then shyly ducked my head. "Thanks, guys," I said. "You really are a great support for me. But I have to be realistic. I've got a real serious decision to make. You can't imagine how bad Medallion looked. Besides, even if John could help him, I'm not sure he can afford him. When we were in San Antonio, he told me he didn't know if he could afford to take on any more horses, least of all one who runs up such big vet bills. I hate to admit it, but it sure feels hopeless."

Elizabeth tugged me into her arms, "One day at a time,"[3] she gently offered. "Let's take this to God. Remember, things may seem impossible to us, but they are not to Him. Let's pray for God to take control of all this." And that's just what we did.

## Dark Days Ahead

**M**om and I met Grandma and Gramps at church the next morning. After a late night with Mark and Elizabeth and sitting in the pew listening to the rain trickle against the stained glass windows, I kept nodding off during the sermon. I awoke when Gramps nudged me just in time to catch Pastor Bryan's summation, "When life throws you a curve ball and you're unsure about what to do…remember Psalms 27:14, 'Wait for the LORD; be strong and take heart and wait for the LORD.'"

Finally, the service ended with everyone singing, "Trust and obey, for there's no other way, to be happy in Jesus, but to trust and obey."

So as hard as all that was, that's exactly what I did. I waited on the Lord, trusting and obeying, well at least as well as I could anyway.

All day I dozed off under the cloudy, drizzly skies. I prayed and waited, even fasted from eating any chocolate until the early evening when Mom dropped me off at Dad's, just in time to share with him what looked like a pretty dismal spring break.

Shaking the rain from my umbrella, I walked on in, grabbing Pooh and giving him a hello kiss behind his ear to calm his barking. I caught the last of Dad's telephone call as I strolled into the kitchen.

"Fine then," he said. "Becky and I will head out before sun up to take one last look at him and help you out with the details. I'm glad you decided to help us out and take the vet's advice to get this done first thing in the morning." Thunder crashed, causing the kitchen window to vibrate.

"Hey, buddy, thanks a lot," Dad added, his voice breaking. "This sure is a hard thing for us to do."

I glanced at my reflection in the window as I clutched Pooh to my heart for comfort. I was as pale as his white coat. Buddy, whoever that guy was, had taken the stupid vet's advice. They were putting Medallion down, first thing in the morning, and I was going down to San Antonio to watch it all. I couldn't believe my ears! The decision was made without me. And at that moment, I hated Dad and that two-faced dream-breaker John. I hated them both for teaching me to hope for miracles.

"Hi, hon." Dad smiled, realizing I heard the final words of his conversation. "What's wrong, sweetie? You look as pale and angry as an old wet hen."

He came around the cabinet to put his arm around me, but I quickly turned and marched to my room, promptly slamming the door so hard the shelf on the wall with all my horse books crashed down to the ground with a *kapow!*

Dad rushed in to see what caused all the commotion. There I stood, my face buried in Pooh's fur, tears streaming down my face, gasping for air between sobs.

"How could you?" I screamed at my father. Pooh squirmed in my arms, touched his wet button nose to my cheek, then started licking the tears on my face to help make me feel better.

"But, sweetheart, I thought that's what you wanted," Dad answered feebly.

"What I wanted? How can you say that? I begged you not to kill him. I begged you to sell Medallion to John. I begged John to buy him. You've both let me down. I ha—"

Before I could get out the words "hate you," Dad broke in, "I sold Medallion to John just like you asked, and at a great price, I must add."

"See, I knew it! You sold him…you…sold him? To John? John bought Medallion to save him? But…but…I thought you said buddy took the vet's advice?"

"He did Becky. John…my buddy, took Dr. Simpson's advice…to try and load Medallion first thing in the morning to bring him to Austin. He thought the stallion would be calmer and the traffic would be lighter on the Monday morning beginning spring break."

Seeing the color coming back into my face and the relief coming back into my eyes, Dad hugged me and whispered, "The challenge has only begun, sweetheart. Now, better get ready for bed. We need to leave out early in the morning, about four o'clock."

# *Onward and Upward*

"Could Mark and Elizabeth come with us, Dad?" I ventured to ask. "I could really use their support."

"We'll be leaving bright and early, remember, Becky?" But seeing the plea in my eyes, he hesitated only a minute, and then said, "Give them a call. I'm sure John's got room for two more. Your friends have to be here within the hour, so we can all hit the hay early tonight and be ready to go before the break of dawn. Here," he said, handing the kitchen phone to me. "You use this one, and I'll alert John on the cell."

Mark and Elizabeth were both thrilled to join the adventure. Before the hour had passed, they were both at the door shaking out their wet ponchos with backpacks and CDs in hand, all ready to go.

John drove up right on time at 4:00 a.m. in his Tundra truck with an extended cab for the extra passengers and his empty two-horse trailer in tow. He honked. The crew all piled out the door of the house and into their proper places. "Hey guys, glad to have your support," John said winking at the passengers in the back. Then he put the truck in forward gear and off we raced.

The rain slowed to occasional drips, and time passed quickly as my friends and I chattered and listened to music in the backseat.

Just after sunup, we arrived at the Simpson's ranch and, hopping out of the truck, made a beeline straight to Medallion.

The horse stopped pacing and came over to blow air on my hand. He actually looked a little better to me. He hadn't had any more incidents since I had seen him on Saturday. And Doc had dressed his wounds well so there was no gushing blood this time.

Of course, seeing Medallion for the first time, Elizabeth gasped and turned white as a ghost. Mark rushed over and wrapped his arms around both of our shoulders, offering comfort.

Doc, Dad, and John joined our group. Doc Simpson's kids followed close behind. "You young'uns go take a look around while we grown-ups size up this here situation," Doc said.

I sure didn't like the way Doc always wanted to dismiss me from the decisions, but because everyone was working so hard to help Medallion, I decided to just zip it and do as I was told.

Turns out Old Doc really did love horses after all. His kids, Tom and Tina, enjoyed showing us all the ones their dad was caring for as well as some that they owned.

"This is my horse, Freckles," Tina proudly announced. "He's an Appaloosa with freckles on his face rather than on his rump." It's said that sometimes dogs look like their owners. I could see a resemblance between horse and owner here since Tina had a whole slew of freckles running across the bridge of her nose.

Tom introduced us to his horse next, a shiny copper-brown sorrel named Buster. "He got his name because of the way he acts, quiet one minute, then a real *buster* the next."

To further explain, Tom mounted up and then trotted around the corral. Sure enough, Buster loped politely for a couple of rounds, then all of a sudden, he started bucking his back legs. "Crow-hopping," Tina called it. Buster wasn't bucking too high, so Tom was never really in danger. But the action caused us to laugh at the funny sight in spite of ourselves.

Tom didn't mind. He thought it made him look like a bronco in the rodeo. He'd hold on to the reins and saddle horn with his left hand and swing his right hand in the air with a yell, "Yahoo!" That's probably why Buster continued to act the part. He knew his rider liked it.

I have to admit, my mind eased a bit during the couple of hours we toured the rest of the ranch. Just before heading back to the house, I spotted a golden palomino out in the field. "Look!" I called to the group, climbing up on the fence railing. "It looks like Medallion's twin."

"Except this *mare's* expecting a colt." Tina introduced us to Buttercup. "It should be born in about a month," she added with a secretive kind of whisper. The mare stopped grazing and held up her head to view the crowd. Ears perked to attention.

"She looks so much like Medallion." I smiled. Then, noticing the pity in Elizabeth's eyes, my smile faded. "Well, it's how he used to look before."

The sun was shining bright, quietly pulling up the last curtain of rain with it. "Breakfast time," Mrs. Simpson called out the back door and rang a triangle made of iron.

I didn't think we should waste time with breakfast, but Dad came up behind me and cleared his throat. "Saved by the bell," he said, rubbing my shoulders and pulling me in for a hug. I think he hoped breakfast with the Simpsons would help us all face the challenges of the day with a bit more strength. So he agreed to take Mrs. Simpson up on her generous offer.

During breakfast, I found out that Doc Simpson was not such a bad guy after all. He really was quite a funny little man, telling jokes all during the meal, opening up his home and family to us all as he had done.

I realized, in spite of Medallion's condition, I was having one of the best times I'd ever had, just being with friends, real friends with whom I could fully trust and be myself.

A couple of hours of rest and good food helped us meet the next challenge of the morning: the loading of Medallion into the trailer.

As John had expected, Medallion wanted nothing to do with loading, mostly because to load, he had to come up close to a *truck*, which was too much like the *car* that had hit him. And whoa, how that horse's mind games began!

The first attempt proved almost disastrous. At first sight of the vehicle, Medallion reared up and clipped John in the face with his front hoof. Then, the horse began snorting and backing up, pulling against the rope.

John sensed immediately there would be serious trouble if he continued to push Medallion into the trailer. So he patiently circled the horse around and took him out to a grassy corral to calm him down before the horse's anger and fear sent him completely out of control. Our counselor was so good with managing anger. I had seen him work it out of my friends and me, and I was sure he could do it with Medallion.

Once in the corral, John whispered to the horse and gently ran his hand over the horse's hide. He worked with Medallion, taking his time for over an hour, till he felt it was time to try it again.

Doc Simpson stood in amazement as he watched a skittish but much calmer Medallion walk to the back of the trailer. The horse plopped one angry hoof on the bed of the trailer, and then slowly he raised the other hoof and slammed it in as well.

*Come on, boy*, I thought as I watched from the house, *you're almost there.*

But just when I thought he would do it, the horse backed out and began pulling back on the reins. Three more times, John let him back out, then circle, and attempt the load again.

I was getting anxious, so I quietly slipped outside and edged my way up closer to the trailer. John saw me and motioned me over. "Talk to him, Becky, slow and easy. Let him know how much you love him and what you expect of him."

Doing just as John instructed, I whispered softly and petted Medallion's face in slow, gentle strokes. Then I moved to the side of the trailer and climbed up on the side step at the front. Dad gave me some oats, which I put in my hand. Then extending my arm inside the window at the front of the trailer, I called, "Come on, Medallion. Come on, boy. Let's go home."

He snorted and nodded his head, then took his first step up into the trailer. This time, however, he didn't stop but came all the way into the oats I extended to him in my hand. He fluttered a warm hello with his nostrils and licked the food from my fingers.

"Onward and upward," John said as he let out a deep sigh and shut the back door of the trailer. It had been a long morning, full of being still, waiting, being patient, and moving slowly; but finally after many hours of trusting and obeying, Dad said, "Get on in, everyone. We're ready to move on."

## Finally Home

By midafternoon, we were back at John's ranch. I used Dad's cell phone to call Mom. I wanted to make sure she was in on everything that was going on, so I begged her to come out, "Please, Mom. I know how you feel about seeing Dad, but you have to face him sometime."

Ever since Dad had remarried, Mom saw as little of him as possible. She said it just hurt too much seeing him, especially with another woman and child. But it had been more than two years, and I was hoping the pain had eased up a bit. Mom finally agreed and said she'd be over as soon as she could.

Now that Mom agreed to come, my stomach tightened with jitters. I had already fought nervousness about unloading Medallion, but that actually turned out pretty good.

This time, John called for my help from the beginning of the unloading procedure to talk Medallion out. At first, he nickered and stomped the floor of the trailer defiantly, but then as I whispered instructions and caressed him on his jaw, he slowly backed on out.

Maybe he was tired from the trip because after unloading, Medallion gave us relatively little trouble. As John took the lead rope and walked ahead, Medallion quietly trotted behind.

John decided to seclude Medallion in a grassy corral near the house so he could work with the horse and keep a close eye on him for a while. When John first put the horse in, Medallion trotted to the feed trough and licked up some leftover grains and then he pranced around the arena nickering at some geldings in a nearby pen as if to say hello. As I watched, my mind eased. I couldn't understand why old Doc Simpson was so worked up; Medallion acted about as normal as he did before we moved from San Antonio. Surely, now that he was here, I could come out and ride him, and everything would be back to normal in no time.

Without warning, Medallion suddenly bolted and started bucking, throwing his whole weight up into the air charging toward the iron rail fence. Only at the last second did he pull up enough to save himself from a massive blow to the chest.

"This is our next big challenge," John told the assembled group but had his eye on me. "Medallion has become totally *unpredictable*." And with that, John swung himself over the rails and slung a lasso around the horse's neck in an effort to calm the beast and ease him through the changes he would now have to face.

*Unpredictable*, there was that word again. As we watched John work his magic with Medallion in the corral, I recalled the discussion John and I had the last time he used that word with me. It was in answer to my question, "Why can't my parents get along?"

"No one can say for sure. However, it appears your dad might be a bit *unpredictable*," John had said during one of our private sessions. "Remember the day he found a boat online, went and bought it and pulled it up to the front door? And then he bought the cabin on the lake to keep the boat. Oh, and my personal favorite," John added with a chuckle, "the llama he bought because it had long eyelashes like yours and spit like your little stepsister used to do with her oatmeal!

"There's nothing wrong with his spontaneity. It can actually be quite exciting. After all, that's how you got Medallion," John reminded me. "Just as long as the one who lives with your Dad understands and thrives on these actions as well.

"Living with someone so unpredictable, however, can be very difficult, especially for someone like your mom, who you described as one who resists change and thinks long and hard before jumping into things, a person who needs to feel more secure. Truthfully, she's a bit more like me.

"My own mother was more of the unpredictable breed as well," John continued. "My parents divorced when I was twelve, but up until then, my life felt like a roller-coaster ride.

"When the arguments between them first started, I felt responsible. If only I could say the right thing, I could stop the arguing. But in reality, I could never stop it. It wasn't until years later when *I* went in for some counseling that I finally began to forgive myself. My mentor said, 'When you get frustrated, try to remember the three Cs. You didn't *cause* it. You can't *control* it. You can't *cure* it.'"[4]

He further explained, "Divorce is not caused by the children, but by things that exist between the couple involved. For various reasons, the couple has become emotionally disconnected."

At that point in the discussion, I thought about Irene, how we had been pretty good friends, but then when I moved away, we just stopped writing to one another and now our friendship was, well…dead.

"It's kind of like that," John continued. "Most friendships like that will slowly draw to a close because there's little emotion that connects them. Things change and they don't.

"To keep any relationship strong, two people have to want the same things very badly and work to keep the love between them strong. They have to take the risk to communicate their feelings like we've done in our group.

"The most important thing you have to remember in all this," John said, "is that the divorce was not your fault. Your parents, both of them, love you dearly. There is no way they want you to feel at blame."

John had spoken with me a number of times to help me sort out my feelings concerning the divorce. I truly felt the healing between my parents, and I was well under way. Very rarely these days did I feel angry with them or myself. I was learning how to forgive.

My two lives had actually become quite fun. With Dad, I enjoyed the new family unit, including Pooh and my new little sister. Kelly was a cute little doll, and I was excited to think I was no longer an only child; now I had a sister.

I hoped one day Mom might find a husband to love, one who could love her just the way she needed. But for right now, she seemed to be enjoying her independence. She was attending to her college courses, and we were growing closer and learning how to work through the changes together, studying, cooking, and playing games together, almost more like friends than mother and daughter.

As I stood on the rails of the fence, watching John quiet Medallion, all these thoughts rolled through my head. Mom's car tires crunched on the gravel behind me. I jumped down and ran to give her a quick hug.

During the past year, John and Mom had become good friends. When she drove up, he waved and smiled, then quickly left Medallion's corral and trotted up to Mom's car.

Surprising both Dad and me, John leaned down and brushed a kiss by Mom's cheek! Though a bit shocked, I accepted the gesture and actually felt quite pleased.

Was life becoming a bit more secure? Maybe. Would it remain *unpredictable*? No doubt.

# Outcomes and Opportunities

It was almost Independence Day. The last few months came and went like a flash, maybe because life was on an uphill swing again.

After Medallion arrived in Austin, there were many days when I had my doubts and so did John. "Becky, I can't promise you miracles," he warned. "I'll hold on to Medallion for a while, and we'll see what kind of progress he's making. Doc was right about mind games Medallion is playing. He's definitely been in a nosedive situation. I've got a few things up my sleeve to try and hopefully, with your help, and God's grace, we can get him going in the right direction again.

"Attitude is as important with horses as it is with humans. They have to believe they can survive. Otherwise, they can literally trample themselves to death. As humans, it's okay to ask for support when things get rough. For horses, they have to have concerned loving adults jump in to help them from time to time as well. We'll take it like we say in group, 'one day at a time.'"

It seemed one of the greatest things John did for Medallion was to fix things so he could run through the back pastureland with a herd. This sure seemed to suit him, almost as much as finding a trusting *herd* of my own helped me. "Look at you shine!" I whispered to the palomino the last time I brushed his golden coat. His mane and tail as well were all grown back and as thick as before the accident.

Though Medallion still wasn't ready for riding, he had fewer and fewer angry outbursts these days. When they came, I understood, knowing myself that healing is a difficult ongoing process.

Mom and Dad were beginning to speak better of each other, though they still felt separate meetings to the ranch were best.

Today, however, was an exception.

Dad, in his unpredictable fashion, had called to say he had a surprise for me. He wanted Mom and my friends to come and share the experience. So here we all were, heading to John's ranch, the warm Texas sun flooding the windows of Mom's car.

When I arrived, Dad and the gang—Marcy, Kelly, and Pooh—were already there. Dad could hardly contain himself. There was a familiar twinkle in his eye.

"Bec, you sure are looking great," teased Dad. "I bet instead of Becky Butter Belly, the kids call you B-e-a-utiful Becky these days." Right around the corner of my thirteenth birthday, I could still be picked up by Dad, especially since I had lost that extra twenty-five pounds, and that's just what he tried to do.

"Put me down, Daaaad." I giggled and squirmed. For that's just what young ladies do when their dads act lame, especially when their friends are there to watch.

"Where's John and what's this big surprise we're all here to see?" I asked, bouncing from one foot to the other.

"Come this way, young lad and ladies," Dad cheered. He turned to march to the stable, a line of curious onlookers trailing close behind.

John opened the door as he heard the group approach. "Look what I found in my stable," he said, pulling on a tiny blue lead rope. Out pranced a colt, as golden as a perfect Texas sunset. It had a stubby white mane and a tail that swished up and down, just waiting to be brushed.

I could hardly believe it! Running to hug him, I cried, "A colt! A palomino colt for my very own! Wait. Is it mine? Could it be mine?" I stammered, my heart racing for a reply. Dad smiled and nodded up and down. I ran to his arms, and he picked me up and twirled me around like a toddler.

Turns out, this was the reason Dad had kept Medallion in San Antonio when we moved, to have him father this colt.

"This is one thing I thought long and hard about doing," Dad said proudly.

"And your dad and I even came to a peaceful agreement about it this time," Mom added. They had made this decision together, thought it out beforehand. A lot had changed in their relationship.

"You've dealt with our bad choices for years, Becky," Dad continued. "We hope you'll accept this gift as our way of saying how much we love you."

"Hey," Mark chimed in, "is this what is meant by a *golden* opportunity?"

"Maybe for us all," Elizabeth added quietly, "a fresh start."

"That's it!" I exclaimed. "My little pony can be named Golden Opportunity. I'll call him Opportunity for short." Patting my new colt, looking around at my family and friends, I choked back tears. Suddenly, I remembered my dream from years ago and that beautiful rainbow. Like a sign, God used nature, magically letting me know, somehow things would be okay. And He had been faithful.

I had prayed to get Medallion back, my dad back, and a new life. Miraculously, all three of my prayers were answered, not exactly in the form I imagined, but perhaps better than I ever dreamed they could be.

## Questions for Thought

### *Horse Dreams*

In the story, the counselor, Mr. Phillips, helps Becky and the other members of her support group by talking through some of the problems they are facing. One thing he encouraged the children to do on their own was to keep a journal to record their thoughts and questions. The questions below could have been similar ones the friends discussed in their group meetings. As the story unfolds, or after reading the book, students, teachers, and parents might use them not only to understand how the characters felt but how we, as readers, feel about the topics as well.

*Chapter 1: Insanity Reigns*

1. The author uses weather to set the mood of the chapter. How does weather affect your mood?
2. Why is the character, who is telling the story, so angry?

3. What does the main character do in this chapter to gain strength?

*Chapter 2: A Momentous Day*

4. What leads Becky to believe she will have a momentous day?
5. In what way does she make it a momentous day?

*Chapter 3: Party on the River*

6. Do a bit of research to find out the approximate cost of Becky's birthday party.
7. Do you think Dad made a wise decision to give Becky this kind of party? Why or why not?

*Chapter 4: Friends*

8. Tell why you would or would not choose to have Sue Ann as a friend.
9. Why did Becky choose Irene as a friend?
10. Why did Irene choose *Dear Mr. Henshaw* to read?

*Chapter 5: My Only Friend*

11. What makes Medallion a good friend for Becky?
12. Why does Becky feel guilty in this chapter? Does she have a reason to feel this way?

*Chapter 6: As the Divorce Turns*

13. How does Mom change after the separation?
14. How does Becky change after the separation?

*Chapter 7: Disappearing Dad*

15. Tell about something good that happens because of the separation.
16. Tell about a time when something bad unexpectedly turned out to be good for you.

*Chapter 8: One Step Forward, Two Steps Back*

17. How does Mom's behavior affect Becky?
18. How does Dad's behavior affect Becky?

*Chapter 9: Uprooted*

19. This chapter is titled "Uprooted." What details from this chapter made Becky feel uprooted? Be sure to think about several details, such as incidents, weather, and surroundings.
20. Name things that could happen in life that would cause children to feel uprooted.
21. What are some things children might have to leave behind when they move to a new place?

*Chapter 10: The Big Move*

22. Name one thing you would have put in your backpack to take along during the move.
23. What are some things that Becky could be looking forward to because of the move?

*Chapter 11: New Surroundings*

24. How was Becky's appetite affected by her feelings?
25. In this chapter, Dad and Mom argue over buying Medallion. Becky mentions the "cause and effect" lessons she learned in school. Discuss cause and effect as they relate to this situation.
26. Do you think it was a good idea for Dad to buy this horse? Tell why or why not.

*Chapter 12: New School, New Support*

27. Do you think Becky needs a support group? Why or why not?
28. What reasons would Mom have for going to a support group?

*Chapter 13: Hanging Out with Dad*

29. Do you think Dad made a good decision when he got Pooh Bear? Discuss what could be good about Dad's decision. What's something bad that could happen because of Dad's decision?

*Chapter 14: In Touch with Medallion*

30. Why would Becky want to stay in the dream?
31. Think about a dream that you've had where you wanted to stay in the dream. Or imagine a dream you would like to stay in. Describe it.

*Chapter 15: The Morning After*

32. Describe the feelings Becky had for her stepmom.
33. Describe the feelings Becky had for Kelly.

*Chapter 16: Back in School*

34. Tell something you do to get ready for the new school year.
35. Why do you think Mark was chosen for the support group?
36. Why do you think Elizabeth was chosen for the group?

*Chapter 17: Real Support*

37. What was the importance of Mr. Phillips sharing with the children the story about the old horse who was put in the pen alone?
38. Tell how an animal you have had, or one you know about, has helped a person.

*Chapter 18: Joining the Herd*

39. Describe your lunchroom similarly to the way the support group talks about theirs.
40. Describe the "invisible" child.

*Chapter 19: Peaceful Leaders*

41. What is the sole purpose of the animal kingdom according to John? Tell why you agree or disagree.
42. Who is a peaceful leader at your school?

*Chapter 20: The Ranch Community*

43. What effect did the ranch community have on the school?
44. Tell about something at your school that helps build community.

*Chapter 21: Trouble in San Antonio*

45. Why did Becky's dad keep news of the accident from her?
46. What effect did Medallion's accident have on the relationship between Becky and her dad?
47. Discuss a change Becky is making to improve her life.

*Chapter 22: Help on the Way*

48. Becky was wondering why bad things had to happen to her. Why do you think bad things happen to people?
49. What did Elizabeth and Becky do to become friends?
50. What things did Becky's mom do to help herself?

*Chapter 23: Put Him Down*

51. How is this chapter similar to chapter 1?
52. Do you think Medallion should have been put down? Why or why not?
53. Who was the one person Becky recalled that had changed her life, and would always remain faithful to her through good times and bad?

*Chapter 24: Down and Out*

54. How did Mark and Elizabeth try to help Becky?
55. Tell about someone you can go to for help when you are hurting.

*Chapter 25: Dark Days Ahead*

56. How does the author use weather to set the mood at the beginning of this chapter?
57. What caused Becky's hope to resurface at the end of this chapter?

*Chapter 26: Onward and Upward*

58. Why do you think the author introduced Buttercup into the story?
59. What characteristics did John have that he could use to help Medallion?

*Chapter 27: Finally Home*

60. Explain what "unpredictable" means in this story.
61. How can quoting the three Cs help people?

*Chapter 28: Outcomes and Opportunities*

62. How did the characters change in this story? What do you think was the single most important thing that caused the change?
63. Do you think Dad made a good decision in getting Opportunity for Becky? Why or why not?
64. Make predictions about what you think will happen to Medallion, Opportunity, and the human characters in this story.
65. If you know someone in need of help, what advice could you give?

## Message of Hope

**You are not alone.**
Change may not be immediate,
but it is one thing in life you can always count on.
You can make change happen by making good choices,
and having the courage
to go *beyond yourself.*
If you need support,
pray first; invite God into your life,
and then search out *responsible* adults,
friends who *have proven* themselves trustworthy,
or use the Internet or even the front of the
yellow pages of a telephone book
where there are *helpful numbers* for every kind of crisis.
For addiction or alcohol-related situations,
call your local Al-Anon/Alateen information organizations.
Most importantly, remember
**You are not alone!**

# *Endnotes*

1. Al-Anon Family Groups, *How Al-Anon Works for Families & Friends of Alcoholics*, (New York: Al-Anon Family Group Headquarters, Inc., 1995), 56.
2. *How Al-Anon Works*, 56.
3. *How Al-Anon Works*, 66.
4. *How Al-Anon Works*, 158.